DISCIPLINE

Randa Abdel-Fattah

ONEWORLD

Book club notes are available at oneworld.co.uk

A Oneworld Book

First published in the United Kingdom, United States, Canada, Ireland and South Africa by Oneworld Publications Ltd, 2026

First published in Australia and New Zealand by University of Queensland Press, 2025

A CIP record for this title is available from the British Library

ISBN 978-1-83643-363-7
eISBN 978-1-83643-364-4

Typeset by Post Pre-press Group, Brisbane
Printed and bound in Great Britain by Clays Ltd, Elcograf S.p.A

The authorised representative in the EEA is eucomply OÜ, Pärnu mnt 139b–14, 11317 Tallinn, Estonia (email: hello@eucompliancepartner.com / phone: +33757690241)

Oneworld Publications Ltd
10 Bloomsbury Street
London WC1B 3SR
England

Praise for *Discipline*

Shortlisted for the Miles Franklin Literary Award

'Discipline is razor sharp, uncompromising and bitingly funny – a brilliant combination.'

Omar Robert Hamilton, author of *The City Always Wins*

'As Ramadan unfolds under the shadow of the Gaza genocide, Discipline asks what is the cost of speaking truth to power, and worse, what is the cost of remaining silent? In this blistering, urgent novel, Randa Abdel-Fattah captures the impossible choices faced by those who dare to raise their voices in a world that demands silence. Unflinching in its moral clarity, this book is necessary reading.'

Susan Abulhawa, author of *Mornings in Jenin*

'This book is so important.'

Jack Edwards, Inklings Book Club founder

'For those who seek to sincerely understand the endless obstacles one must face in the body of an Arab, a Palestinian, a Muslim, *Discipline* is the place to begin.'

Michael Mohammed Ahmad, author of *The Other Half of You*

'An unflinching dive into the fractures of our social fabric… With razor-sharp insight, this brilliant and captivating novel is a fierce cry for action.'

Samah Sabawi, author of *Cactus Pear for My Beloved*

'Randa Abdel-Fattah is a remarkable writer. With humility and care she asks that we do not turn away from the people of Gaza. *Discipline* is a novel that reminds us that each story is a shared story, demanding our attention. *Discipline* is an invitation to be in this world together.'

Tony Birch, author of *The White Girl*

'Blistering and brilliant.'

Melissa Lucashenko, author of *Edenglassie*

I humbly dedicate this book to all the Palestinian academics and journalists killed in Gaza who would be alive now if academics and journalists in the West had spoken and acted when they had the chance.

1

He pressed call, staring at the rose that was her WhatsApp profile picture as he waited for her to respond.

She answered, 'Assalamu—' Then it cut out, as often happened with the internet connection in the village on the outskirts of Aden she'd been living in for the last year.

He waited five minutes and then dialled again.

'Assalamu Alaikom, Ashraf. They're just coming inside.'

Mya had forgotten to turn off the video. Her curly Egyptian hair was longer now, past her shoulders, still in coils and spirals. He used to twirl them around his fingers. She looked thinner, her collarbones clearly protruding. She was still as lovely as he remembered her.

Out of respect, he considered telling her the video was on. But to do so would be to submit to the absurdity of a situation he refused to legitimise. For God's sake, they'd been a high school couple, married for nineteen years. He knew every part of her body. And yet, it was for God's sake now that she covered her hair in front of him.

Because they were divorced.

'Years you called me Ash,' he said. 'Do you score more points with God if you call me Ashraf now?'

Mya shot him a withering look.

'So, how are you?' he asked.

'Alhamdullilah.'

'And how's your husband?'

'Do you really want to know?'

'I asked, didn't I?'

'He's working long hours. There aren't enough doctors.'

'Is he treating Layla and Shaymaa well?'

'You know very well he is. They adore him.'

'Really? Don't teenagers hate everybody? He deserves to be congratulated.'

'Oh! AstaghfurAllah!' Mya's camera turned off suddenly.

He couldn't help but roll his eyes. Why did religion make such fools of people? 'I'm a different person now,' she'd explained the first time she'd worn a hijab in front of him after the divorce two years ago. In a way, she was right. The Mya he'd married knew her wines, loved to party, took pride in getting dressed up and was rising to the top of the corporate banking ladder. He didn't recognise this woman. Hadn't recognised her for several years now. This woman who memorised the numbers of food additives that contained gelatine, replaced make-up and short skirts with a black hijab and shapeless abaya, quit her job, insisted they sell their mortgaged house to rent because interest was a sin and threw herself into charity work. This woman who had divorced him, married a doctor with a beard down to his chest and moved with their daughters and her new halal-certified husband, Abdel-Karim, to a village in Yemen.

She was back on the screen now, adjusting a scarf around her head. 'You should have said something, Ashraf.'

'Nothing I haven't seen, or touched, before.'

'You're impossible. Are you fasting?'

'No.'

'Allah yahdeek. Here, speak to Layla and Shaymaa.'

The girls appeared in the frame. He felt a pang and touched their faces on the screen.

They still had their strong Sydney accents. Layla prattled on about juggling her online studies with coaching a soccer team at the orphanage Mya was managing. Shaymaa sat quietly, occasionally interrupting to enquire about his health and Snowball the cat. (He didn't have the heart to tell her Snowball had also run away.)

'Maria says hi,' Ashraf said. 'She's drowning in exam prep. I bumped into her at the shops.'

'Yeah, I know,' Layla, his youngest, said. 'She Snapped me.'

'Oh, okay. It's good you're staying in touch with your friends.'

'It's called wi-fi, Dad,' Layla said. 'We're overseas, not on the moon.'

'She's killing it with her assessments,' Shaymaa said. 'She'll get the marks to do med, InshAllah. Hey, are you in a hotel room, Dad?'

'Yes. Melbourne. A boring conference. So, what about your studies?'

'Few more months,' Shaymaa said.

'Then?'

'Teaching course. We spoke about this.'

Ever since he could remember, Shaymaa had wanted to be an engineer. That goal had now been rejected for ideological reasons. Teaching is a more female-friendly profession, she'd insisted, parroting Mya, when they spoke last. He'd tried to push back – you couldn't take a step anywhere in the Muslim world without finding a woman engineer – but soon conceded defeat. He couldn't play parent via video calls. He'd been reduced to being an online spectator of their lives. For all her talk about 'feminism eroding traditional family structures' and 'patriarchy offering families security', Mya had certainly done a number on him.

'Don't stress, Dad,' Shaymaa said. 'We're happy.'

She smiled so genuinely that it hurt his insides. Where was her bitterness about the entire upheaval of her life? Some adolescent rebellion and rage? He was ashamed to admit that he felt disappointed that she seemed so content. That she was reminding him that he seemed to be the only person who was aching about the fact that his daughters had been whisked away to Yemen to live out some religious-inspired utopian fantasy of their mother's.

'How's Ramadan, Dad?' Layla asked.

'Ramadan Mubarak, habibti.'

‘Please, Dad. Fast, pray. Please. Praying’s the line between Islam and kufr.’

‘InshAllah,’ Ashraf said robotically.

He didn’t bother protesting or arguing. InshAllah from his lips was nuanced enough to convey his feelings on the subject. And his daughters’ resigned sighs were enough to convey that they understood too.

2

Sirens blasted from Holroyd Road at the exact same time as Hannah's alarm blared. She jolted up and, terrified of rousing Aya, quickly silenced the alarm with one hand and reached out to shake Jamal awake with the other. He didn't stir.

'Yala,' she coaxed, shaking him again.

Waking up for suhoor before sunrise was never easy, but *My God*, she thought, *this morning is an act of jihad.* This was Hannah and Jamal's second Ramadan as a married couple and their first as exhausted parents.

Aya had been unsettled and needed a night feed, although it was more accurately described as a nibble. She'd had to wean Aya as she approached the return to work, so now, after two months back and with Aya on the bottle and solids during the day, her supply had declined significantly.

Last night's feed had ended with Aya falling asleep on Hannah's breast and Hannah, wide awake, scrolling on her phone for another half an hour hooked to the headlines, tweets, TikTok videos and posts from Palestine: Israeli mobs in East Jerusalem attacking protesters outside their homes – scroll – Muna al-Kurd's anguished cry, 'You are stealing my house!' – scroll – tear gas and gunfire on worshippers at Al Aqsa.

Hannah knew she shouldn't look while she was breastfeeding, knew that the stress would pass through her milk. But how could she look away?

She struggled to go back to sleep after suhoor and ended up staying awake, guiltily watching *Emily in Paris* instead of reading the Quran until it was past time to get ready for work.

She showered, put on a pair of pants that she could finally fit into thanks to three weeks of fasting, slicked back her long, keratin-straightened hair into a high ponytail and attempted to cover her exhausted face in some make-up.

She remade the bed because Jamal, who was now in the shower, never got the edges and pillow angles right, and then tiptoed into Aya's room to check on her.

Aya was awake and, on locking eyes with Hannah, let out an ear-splitting cry.

Hannah leant over the cot, trying not to take a breath, but there was no defence. The smell of shit was too strong. She ripped off her suit jacket, threw it onto the feeding chair.

'It's okay, habibti,' she said, but Aya was beyond soothing reassurances and only cried harder.

Hannah reached down into the cot. She picked Aya up, not realising that the nappy was only half on. It slipped off into the cot, runny shit sliding down Aya's legs and then seeping into the mattress. It was typical that the mattress protector, which had been on the mattress for weeks, was now flapping dry on the washing line the one morning it had a job to do.

'Shit!'

Hannah extended her arms out and tried to hold Aya away from her work clothes. She called out to Jamal, but whether he couldn't hear her because of the shower or because of Aya's screaming was moot.

At fourteen months, Aya was a heavy baby. Hannah had no choice but to lower Aya back into the cot, adding confusion to her discomfort and sending her into a fit of even louder wails.

'Sorry, sorry, sorry! Habibti, you'll drip over the carpet! Just let me go get a towel.'

She ran down the hall as Siri's voice reverberated from her Apple watch: 'Message from John Williams: Al-Bayinnah College. Huge story. Peter's on it. I'd like you to work with him. Get there ASAP. We need your community's first-hand perspective.'

'Are you kidding me?' Hannah yelled into the linen cupboard as she rummaged for an old towel.

She raced back to Aya, picked her up with the towel, held her away from her clothes while uttering a stream of *I'm sorry*s, *ya habibti*s and *ya hayati*s and raced to the main bedroom, where she kicked open the door to the ensuite, threw the shower door open and shoved the baby – dirty towel and all – into her husband's arms.

'Ya omri!' Jamal cooed, but then his eyes and nose took in the scene. 'Aww, ya omri, what happened?'

Aya was winding down, taking double breaths.

'I have to leave,' Hannah said over the gushing water.

She ran back to Aya's room to grab her work jacket, then dashed back again to the ensuite.

'There's a disaster in the cot. Just throw it all in the bin before you take her to Mum's. Are you teaching today or working from home?'

Hannah was working at the paper part-time now, three days a week, and given Jamal was doing his PhD at Joseph Banks University full-time they needed her mother to look after Aya on Hannah's workdays.

'I'm going in to the office to finish working on a chapter,' Jamal called back. 'Is Aya's bag downstairs?'

'On the table. Don't forget to pack her water bottle. It's in the dishwasher. I've really got to go now.' She was turning to leave when she suddenly remembered. 'Shit.'

'Yeah, a lot of it,' Jamal quipped through the steam.

'No, Mum's organised to take Aya out today to visit an old family friend – you know Um Taher.'

Her mother had given her strict instructions: 'dress up Aya' so she could 'show off' her grandchild.

'Put her in the navy-and-white Dior dress with the collar,' Hannah said.

It was a gift from a friend. There was no way Hannah could afford Dior Kids and, even if she could, no way she would be pretentious enough to spend two hundred dollars on a dress that would end up covered in pureed apple and carrot stains.

'It should be on the right side of the cupboard behind the purple jacket.'

'And if I can't find it?'

'You're capable of doing a PhD. Find it.'

Jamal, clearly conceding the point, started singing to Aya.

Hannah walked over to the shower, opened the door and kissed Aya on the cheek. 'I'm so sorry, baby girl. I have to go to work.'

'Stop with the apologies,' Jamal said.

'Yes, yes, I'm living the feminist dream,' Hannah replied as her phone started ringing.

3

Ashraf was bored. It was the final day of the conference in Melbourne on political ideologies in the Arab World, and he was yet to hear anything new or exciting. What was more sobering was the realisation that he was just as bored, if not more so, by his own paper ('Egypt: The road from Nasser to Tahrir Square').

He had been around the Middle East and political science traps for a decade now and most faces were familiar to him. Brendan Nickson was over at the buffet, hogging the vegetarian mini quiches as he regaled a wide-eyed young PhD student with stories about his ethnographic fieldwork in Tripoli. Shivansh Murli was at the podium, fiddling with his PowerPoint for the upcoming plenary, looking as flustered as usual. He had the frenetic energy of a post-grad presenting for the first time, even though it was obvious to everybody that he'd been rehashing the same paper for years now and hadn't formed an original idea since the trade publication of his PhD.

Standing in line for a cup of lukewarm coffee and a gluten-free brownie, Ashraf regretted not bringing a jacket.

The convention centre was doing an excellent job of burning the planet in order to run the air-conditioning at uncomfortably cold levels as they all discussed decolonial approaches to climate change. He was depending on that coffee to restore some warmth to his body.

Ashraf scrolled through the latest updates on *Al Jazeera*. Israeli forces had stormed the Al-Aqsa Mosque compound firing stun grenades, live ammunition and tear gas into the crowds gathered for the last Friday prayer of Ramadan.

He switched to *news.com.au* and started scrolling.

He paused at a headline.

Terror in Our Schools: Year 12 Al-Bayinnah College student arrested

He opened the link.

NSW Police have today arrested several activists, including 18-year-old Muslim-Palestinian Year 12 student Nabil Mostafa.

Yesterday evening the activists, wearing 'Free Gaza' t-shirts and keffiyehs, occupied the Centre of Excellence in Artificial Intelligence at Joseph Banks University demanding the centre cut ties with Elbit Systems.

The activists, who belong to the radical direct-action climate group Weapons of Mass Interruption, barricaded and occupied the entrance and painted the walls and doors of the Centre, resulting in thousands of dollars of damage. Mostafa streamed the occupation on his Instagram account.

Wielding a Hamas flag, Mostafa was also wearing a green headband printed with Arabic numbers translating as: '1983, 38, 17'. Comments on the livestream identified this as a reference to the 1983 UN General Assembly resolution on armed struggle.

The paramilitary wing of Hamas, the Izz al-Din al-Qassam Brigades, has been listed as a terrorist organisation since 5 November 2003. There are growing calls for Hamas in its entirety to be listed as a terrorist organisation including from concerned groups such as the Zionist Executive Association of Australia.

While police have not yet charged the protesters, according to ANU Professor of Middle Eastern Studies and deradicalisation expert Jason McCabe advocating support of a terrorist organisation is an offence under Australia's terror laws.

According to the Social Cohesion Policy Institute, 'There is a serious threat to vulnerable Muslim teenagers of being recruited to extremist causes.'

Despite this growing threat, parents at Al-Bayinnah College told *The Daily Story* that the college's principal, Fayza Sayid, refused to address 'worrying and disturbing trends of extremism' in her school.

One parent, who asked to remain anonymous, said that Friday sermons 'disproportionately focused on overseas conflicts like Palestine' and that this 'got the kids worked up about things happening overseas when they should be focused on being Aussies'.

A spokesman for NSW Premier Matthew Dean said: 'We expect all schools identified as having at-risk populations to cooperate with the government's countering violent extremism programs.

'These programs have been created by experts with the input and cooperation of the community.'

Ms Sayid declined to comment.

Ashraf skimmed the article again. He wanted to be sure he'd read correctly. Was this really happening at Fayza's, his ex-wife's sister's, school?

He bookmarked the article, stepped forward in the queue, grabbed his coffee and brownie and went looking for a quiet spot in the convention centre to sit and search for more news.

A colleague intercepted him and suggested they pop into the seminar room next door for the launch of Faye Nickel's new book, *Beneath the Veil in 21st-Century Egypt: Muslim women speak out*. For a few moments he toyed with the idea. It was the least he could do, given he and Faye were in the same university department? And yet he couldn't bring himself to sit through it.

Faye had grown up in Yass, for crying out loud. He'd once asked her: why Middle Eastern politics? She said she'd backpacked through Jordan and Egypt in her gap year and 'fallen in love with Arabs'. 'All of them? Or a specific number?' was his response, to which she replied, without a beat, 'Bedouins.' Faye had returned from her gap year with enough Egyptian dialect to order food and remark on the weather. She enrolled in an arts degree, majoring in political science.

While she'd been teaching introductory units and convening reading groups for eager post-docs naive enough to think there was a job market for them, she'd also been building up her academic CV. Now an associate professor, Faye had just won a lucrative three-year grant to research the role of pottery and music in 'countering violent extremism' among Muslim children in Sydney and London. As far as Ashraf knew, Faye had no background in art or music, and her PhD had been on female genital mutilation.

To hell with collegiality. No, he wouldn't be attending her launch.

Ashraf skolled his coffee as he tried to find more reports online. There was nothing.

He could, he supposed, reach out to Fayza. Check in. It wouldn't have to be awkward, except he hadn't been in touch with her for at least six months. She, too, had been left confused, hurt, angered by Mya's decision. The two of them had nothing in common anymore except their respective disappointment – Fayza as a sister, Ashraf as an ex-husband.

Instead, he sent a text message to Mya: *Have you heard from Fayza? A student at her school's been arrested. All over the media.* It was in the middle of the night in Aden. Ashraf wasn't expecting an immediate response.

He tossed his coffee cup into a bin.

Stuff it, he thought. He had two hours before his panel presentation and he couldn't bear to sit through Shivansh reading out slabs of interview quotes. The man had no idea of the existence of ellipses.

Ashraf would go for a quick swim in the hotel pool and be back in time to present on the role of digital publics in the January uprising. The topic was ironic, given he'd only opened a Twitter account two years ago at the urging of the university's research department. He had some thirty followers and managed to attract a retweet about once a month.

Academics needed to get out there more, apparently. Contribute to policy and public debates, offer a bridge between the public and the academy – *but remember to make your bio catchy*.

Just as soon as he'd written 'Muslim Musings on the Middle East' in the bio field, he'd deleted it and simply put 'Academic, Politics'.

It was all so unbearable.

4

Roadworks and a lane closed on the M4.

'Shit!' Hannah said as she merged into the slow-moving lane.

It was too late to take another route now. She banged her hand on the steering wheel as she considered: *Does swearing invalidate my fast? Is my repentance sincere given that I'm never going to make it to Al-Bayinnah in time, John is going to crack it, my day is only going to get progressively worse and the chances of me swearing aga—*

'Fuck!' Hannah slammed her foot on the brake as a motorbike dived in front of her and then, blocked by traffic, stopped. She leant out of the window and yelled, 'Dickhead!'

The driver didn't bother looking back, merely stuck his middle finger up at her.

Hannah didn't trust herself. She closed her window and shouted at her phone: 'Hey Siri, tell Jamal no way is my fast going to be accepted today, I hate Sydney traffic, how's Aya, why should we pay tolls when the M4 is slower than the main roads, I forgot to take out the chicken to defrost, take it out please.'

Hannah glanced down at her phone, which glowed with her dictated message, but it wasn't Jamal's name that appeared on the screen. It was Sirin's. Hannah hadn't spoken to Sirin in a year, not since she'd subtweeted Hannah, accusing her of being a Labor Party shill and race-traitor because she'd written an article interviewing Muslims about their voting preferences in safe Labor seats.

'Don't send!' she cried. 'Cancel! Hey Siri! Don't send!'

Too late. The swishing sound of a sent text.

'No!'

She just wanted coffee. She didn't know how she would get through the day. Stupid Emily the kafir in Paris with her baguettes and café au lait. Why had she been such an idiot and stayed up? She wanted caffeine so badly she felt like crying.

Hannah streamed *Al Jazeera* news through her car's Bluetooth, struggling to hear over the loud exhaust on the car next to her. She looked over at the driver. He had a mullet and could barely see over the dashboard of his Audi A5. Hannah turned up the volume.

There was a fire of disruption and protests, a 'unity intifada' they were calling it, that had spread across Palestine. In Jerusalem, there were Palestinians fighting back against Israeli settlers who were chanting 'Death to Arabs' as they paraded through the streets. Other Palestinians were fighting back against Israeli soldiers who were storming the Al-Aqsa holy compound. And in the Jerusalem suburb of Sheikh Jarrah, Palestinian families and protesters were fighting back against Israeli forces who were attacking them for demonstrating against Jewish settler groups evicting and confiscating their homes and properties.

Hannah gripped the steering wheel tighter when she heard the newsreader mention uprisings in Lydd, where her father's family had been expelled from in 1948, and also in Kafr Qassem and Kafr Kanna – all villages and towns that were looted and stolen in 1948. Even Nablus, Hebron, Jenin and Ramallah in the West Bank were in revolt. Hannah felt her insides twisting into a pretzel.

She switched to talkback radio. She needed to get her head out of Palestine and focus on a different kind of stress, on the shitstorm here, and there was nobody who produced shitstorms better than Jay Hazley. It was incredible how instantly and intensely his shrill voice triggered her. His fury seemed to travel from the radio straight into her body.

'What's the Australian Security Intelligence Organisation doing about these schools?' he screeched. 'Our tax dollars are paying for these hotbeds of junior jihadis! More Shakespeare and less Shariah is what we need! What's a kid— Excuse me, he's not a kid: he's an adult! Eighteen! What's he doing out of school proudly holding a *Khamas* terrorist flag and with those socialist ratbags? Our laws need changing!'

Almost an hour of traffic later, Hannah pulled into a visitor's parking spot at Al-Bayinnah College in Yagoona. It was a white, red and brown building on a corner block, flanked by a motor repairs shop on one side and an Indian mixed goods store on the other.

It was just after nine and she had missed the media scrum. Any reporters who had been there were long gone, including her senior colleague Peter Henderson, who joined *The Chronicle* while she was on maternity leave.

She had started at *The Chronicle* as a cadet, straight out of uni, five years ago. Her parents had thrown a barbecue with their Palestinian and Lebanese family friends in celebration. (The three-tiered chocolate cake had been decorated with Hannah's photograph and the *Al Jazeera* logo.) Even at twenty-one, she'd known full well that the voices of her community would follow her into every story, every headline, every editorial meeting.

As she approached the ornate black and bronze iron gate and walked down a tiled path into the school grounds, she felt the burden of representation like a medallion around her neck. The hotbed of junior jihadis was quiet. The students were inside their classrooms. Hannah followed the signs to the office, stepping over a Taylor Swift lunchbox lying forgotten on the grass.

Two high school girls emerged from the toilet block, their long bottle-green pleated skirts brushing the floor. Their lips were pouting with freshly applied gloss. One of them adjusted her white scarf, glanced at her, vaguely interested. The other girl snapped her gum and looked Hannah up and down, unsubtle in the way that teenagers are.

Hannah passed by a classroom, catching a glimpse of the class inside. Did they know that they were the subject of the morning's headlines? Did they know that their bodies, names, uniforms, school space had been transformed into dangerous sensory data, imbued with suspicion and panic? A young pimply kid stared at her out the window, boredom written all over his face. The sun through the window lit the poster behind him: advancement, faith, excellence.

Hannah continued on her way to the office, her mind beating with anxiety over the morality of her presence at the school. She sincerely believed she was there to make a difference to how these students and their school would be covered. And yet, it often occurred to her that the industry phrase – *cover a story* – connoted concealing, obscuring, shielding. How could she reconcile this with her conviction that her purpose in this job was to *un*cover? To expose and lay bare, open space for truth and facts by revealing the workings of power? And why was she such a naive fool looking for poetic justice in an industry that was driven by a corporate model of subscriptions and advertising?

They were using her, expecting her to manoeuvre herself into Al-Bayinnah via her Muslimness and Arabness, her contacts and networks. That is, after all, what John had texted her: *We need your community's first-hand perspective.*

How magnanimous John could be. How thoughtful and considerate.

Coffee, she just wanted coffee.

She stopped at a mural of student artwork (the kaabaa, a pencilled sketch of Tupac, a fruit bowl) outside the art room, next door to the front office.

She peeked into the window of the art room and grinned. Among the paintings, sculptures, kilns and pottery were two mannequins, a man and a girl. The man sported a roughly drawn-on beard and thobe, blonde hair slightly exposed under a black turban, and the girl was dressed in a pink Barbie tutu, opaque pink stockings and a keffiyeh as a hijab, holding a small Palestine flag.

The front office was a scene of chaos. A phone was ringing. A tall and striking young woman – flawless make-up, beige turban, brown bodycon, tan heels – was standing at the door of what looked like the sick bay, gently reassuring a pale-looking child who was lying on the bed inside that his aunt was on the way.

Hannah stood back from the reception desk, patiently waiting for a short, chubby receptionist, name tag Salma, to finish signing in a student on an iPad.

The phone wouldn't stop shrilling. Through a door left only slightly ajar, she could hear a man and a woman bickering over who would answer it: 'I'm not speaking to any more media,' 'But what if it's a parent or an important call?'

Salma let out an exasperated cry and answered the phone. 'There's no need to worry,' she said in a reassuring tone that didn't match her frown. 'Yes, they're safe. No, there's no more media here. Yes, it's still a normal school day, same pick-up time. Please don't stress. Ms Sayid has it all under control.'

She hung up, ushered the student out of the office with a firm warning to be on time tomorrow, and faced Hannah. Rubbing her temples, she drew a breath and then said, 'Yes, how can I help you?' Her dangly earrings brushed against her maroon hijab.

Hannah felt her stomach churn. 'Assalamu Alaikom,' she managed with a feeble smile.

Salma returned the greeting of peace through barely contained frustration.

'I'm here to see the school principal. I'm a journalist with *The Chronicle*—'

'Absolutely not!' Salma said, releasing an angry groan. 'You'll need to please leave school premises.'

'I'm Muslim, I'm not here to …' Hannah could feel herself cringing. Why should they believe her?

A door behind her swung open. Hannah turned around and saw, standing framed in the doorway, a woman so regal, so stately, that she almost lost her nerve. She would have walked out of her own volition if the woman, who could only be Ms Sayid, hadn't made the first move.

Ms Sayid said, 'I'm sorry, but I don't care if you're Muslim.'

Ms Sayid's tone wasn't nasty, just firm.

'This is a school, not a media circus. I appreciate you're doing your job. But I would like to do mine, and that means protecting my students and my school.'

There was nothing Hannah could say that would persuade Fayza to budge. The best she could do was offer the principal her business card – 'If you need anything … If you eventually want to talk' – which Ms Sayid accepted the way one would accept a pamphlet from a salesperson hustling dodgy skincare products at a shopping centre kiosk.

5

Ashraf didn't believe in easing oneself into a pool. He strode over to the edge, dived in and immediately felt his body struggle against the shock of the cold.

He pushed through the discomfort, one arm over the other, faster and faster. By the time he touched the wall and somersaulted into another lap, his body relaxed and he gave himself to the water.

Lap after lap he powered on. The black line was his friend, focusing his emotions. He had to face the truth. He'd lost all sense of purpose. How would he face his performance review tomorrow back in Sydney?

He'd failed to receive a grant for quite a few years now. His academic work was too, well, 'academic'. The selection committees were looking for 'impact factor' beyond the academy. His weariness could easily be mistaken for cynicism when actually it was just that he didn't know what it meant to be fulfilled anymore.

Knowledge production in the academy no longer seemed to be enough. What was his 'impact factor'? It was a question that Dean of Political Science Barnaby Williams was sure to ask him in his review.

He had no idea how he would respond.

Ashraf lost his temper during question time for his panel.

Some young Muslim guy wearing a black cap with 'ACAB' printed on it and a black Nike tracksuit, a PhD student and therefore clearly still in the I-am-a-Marxist stage, claimed that Ashraf was 'perpetuating a bourgeoisie, racist, capitalist, Islamophobic, anxious narrative about Hamas as terrorist bogeyman'.

Ashraf allowed him to rant on about the ruling class, Western state terrorism, colonisation and US puppet regimes, but then the guy whipped out an accusation of honorary whiteness.

'I'm going to stop you right there,' Ashraf said, raising his hand. 'Colonisation doesn't explain every problem in the Muslim world. Why is it that in Egypt, where I was born, I have to bribe several people in order to obtain the most basic of documents or services? Or why in Lebanon, where my mother was born, are there no functional basic services?'

Ashraf could feel his face getting hot.

Buoyed by some audience members vigorously nodding, he continued: 'So long as we have young Muslims in complete denial about the abject fatalism of Muslim societies, and so long as Muslims continue to deflect responsibility and blame the West for every ill in their world, Muslims will get the leaders they deserve.'

He hadn't expected applause. He was surprised by how good it made him feel.

The young guy stood up and stormed out of the room.

'Don't let them get to you, Ash,' said his co-panellist Adelaide Jenkins (specialty: Libya).

He smiled. How naive she was to think his anger was about hurt feelings. Like so many white academics in the field, she didn't understand what was at stake. Didn't appreciate the weight of personal history and the costs borne by people such as his family to escape self-defeating ignorance and backwardness.

To think that this angry student – just a kid, really – who hadn't even been conceived when Ashraf's father lost everything in Egypt in the seventies or when his mother escaped the Lebanese civil war ... To think he dared to presume to lecture him. It was the arrogance, the self-indulgent righteousness of this new generation that incensed him. It threatened everything and everybody.

6

It was just after lunch by the time Hannah made it back to the office. She sat at her desk and scanned the coverage.

Al-Bayinnah and Nabil had been elevated from local story to national media storm. Righteous fury oozed from the political and media commentators across the country.

Hamas! Terrorists! Australian values! Western civilisation! Working with the community! Countering violent extremism policies! The Middle East conflict! Social cohesion!

There were op-eds sounding the alarm over radicalisation in Muslim communities and defunding faith-based – especially Islamic – schools. Shock jocks still frothing about why the government had not yet listed the entirety of Hamas as a terrorist organisation. Politicians demanding law reform to ban the public display of flags and political symbols of proscribed organisations. Counterterrorism experts and youth-studies academics posting long, earnest threads on social media with links to their articles in paywalled publications.

Hannah shut her laptop in disgust. She grabbed her phone and texted Jamal, checking in again. He replied that he'd had to cancel his plans on campus and stay home with Aya, whose poo explosion that morning had turned into gastro. She prayed the poosplosion was just a twenty-four-hour bug and that she wouldn't need to take tomorrow off to stay home with Aya. It was the last thing she needed.

In the two months since she'd returned from maternity leave, she could not escape the perception – though no-one would ever admit to it – that she was less valuable and productive as a junior journalist now she was a mother working part-time. And she didn't have much hope it would change, either – no matter how many in-house workshops on gender equality or 'breaking the bias' her senior colleagues completed.

In all honesty, she'd first sensed a shift when she'd married Jamal two years ago, aged twenty-four. It was in the subtle digs about whether it was a 'visa marriage' because he was from Palestine and on a student visa at Joseph Banks University, where they'd met in her last month at uni. Then, when she announced her pregnancy, there were the comments about 'taking care' not to let a baby 'impact' her career just as she was 'getting started'.

She was sandwiched between racism and sexism by people who gave speeches at International Women's Day breakfasts and pasted Acknowledgements of Country in their email signatures.

A WhatsApp notification popped up – an invitation from a friend, Jeanette, to a new group chat focused on the Australian media and their reporting on Gaza. The names were all familiar to her, a network of activists, artists, lawyers and academics involved in Palestine advocacy. She could see Jamal had just been added too. Jeanette was putting them all in touch 'to centralise our efforts, collaborate, share and work together'. She accepted the invitation.

'Hi Hannah.'

Hannah looked up to see Peter hovering over her cubicle.

'Have you had any luck tracking down anybody close to Nabil and his family?'

Hannah placed her phone on her desk. 'Um … no. I was knocked back at the school.'

'You'd tell me if you did?' Peter attempted a cheeky tone that Hannah humoured with a weak smile. 'I've had a bit of a dig,' he said, 'and his socials are all deactivated.'

'So I guess we need my ethnic Rolodex?' Hannah quickly covered up her sarcasm with a forced laugh. She didn't want to get Peter offside. 'I'll try,' she said.

Peter nodded, satisfied. 'I'll put in a word with John to share the byline if you can get somebody in his inner circle on the record. It'll be a massive scoop.'

Hannah felt her stomach sink. There was only one possible direction this story would be allowed to take, and she wanted no part of it. And yet she was in no position to be uncooperative.

Peter pushed his curly fringe back off his small forehead and, to Hannah's annoyance, sat in the chair in the empty cubicle next to her. He rested one foot on his opposite knee, revealing hairy white legs and socks printed with photos of a tabby cat.

'Is that your cat?' Hannah asked, pointing to his sock.

He smiled. 'Yes. Lucy.'

'Cute.'

'I've been in touch with a teacher,' Peter said, caressing his sock, 'from Al-Bayan and—'

'Al-Bayinnah,' she corrected him.

'—she wants to go on the record,' he continued, 'about some of the religious extremism she witnessed at the school when she was teaching there.'

'She's not there anymore?'

'No, they didn't keep her past her probation.'

'Oh,' she said, when what she wanted to say was: *You don't think an ex-teacher who didn't pass probation might have an agenda?* 'What exactly does she mean by extremism anyway?' Hannah felt her voice rising and, with every ounce of self-control, managed to steady it. 'What, I mean …' She tried again, 'What's the evidence of that?'

'She says that students would start loudly reciting the Koran in class, just randomly, when they were in trouble, or yelling out Allahu Akbar knowing it scared her. She said she found it quite threatening and that when she raised it with the coordinator she didn't take her seriously.'

What would Peter say if she told him about her five-year-old nephew, Adam, who had a habit of screaming, 'Allahu Akbar!' as he jumped on the trampoline and loudly yelling, 'Bismillah al Rahman al Raheem!' as he smashed his PJ Masks figurines together in battle?

'I think the story would be more balanced,' Peter said earnestly, 'if we could find some students or parents who can speak to the culture of the school, in terms of religious extremism and whatnot.'

'I don't understand this angle, Peter,' she said. 'Nabil was making a political statement.'

'He started the livestream with *basmallah*.'

Hannah winced at Peter's language butchery, but she forced herself to remain calm. 'The numbers on his headband were a clear legal reference and the colour green was him being subversive. Shock-horror: an activist being a shit-stirrer.'

'Hamas is a terrorist organisation.'

'Well, you'll find most resistance movements are until history decides they're freedom fighters.'

Peter sat up, disappearing Lucy back up his pant leg. 'Do you support Hamas, Hannah?' he spluttered.

Hannah sighed. 'If you sat with my husband's family in Gaza, you'd find some are communist, some are anti-Hamas, some are pro-Hamas, some are Fatah, some are Marxist, some are Islamic Jihad, others Salafi.' She could see Peter's eyebrows rising with every word. 'But all share one thing in common: they're refugees on their own land, living under brutal Israeli occupation and blockade, and they support the right to resist and defend themselves.'

'That doesn't answer my question,' Peter said.

'Not in the way you want it to.'

There was a moment of silence between them, interrupted by Hannah letting out a short, forced laugh in an attempt to defuse the tension.

'Anyway, all I'm saying,' Hannah ventured, 'is that I don't understand why we're assuming the school had anything to do with Nabil's involvement in the protest. It seems a stretch.'

'I agree,' Peter replied, to Hannah's surprise. 'I don't want to assume that Nabil's radicalisation represents all the students. That's why we need more intel to do justice to the story. That's why you need to work on getting insider contacts.'

Hannah felt as if she might explode and, at the exact same time, she wondered what Peter would make of her thinking about exploding. The realisation that it had come to this – to evaluating her private thoughts through a white gaze – was nauseating.

She opened her drawer and rummaged for some painkillers. She pulled out a blister pack and was about to pop out a tablet when Peter, watching her with genuine concern, asked, 'Aren't you fasting?'

Wallahi, by the ninety-nine names of Allah.

Hannah fought back the urge not to punch him in the face. Closing her eyes, she took a deep breath and put the Panadol back in the drawer.

'Yes, momentarily forgot,' she said. And she had. And Peter the fuckwit had been the one to rescue her from breaking her fast.

Peter gave her a sympathetic half-smile.

The white magnanimity was threatening to choke her today.

7

Ashraf's boss, Barnaby, sat in front of a floor-to-ceiling cabinet lined with books and journals on the Cold War. 'Your last grant was six years ago,' he said, thick legs crossed, glasses slipping down his bulbous nose.

'Not for want of applying,' Ashraf replied.

Barnaby flipped through the papers on his desk. 'However, your track record in the past couple of years has been quite solid,' he murmured.

'Divorce has a way of making some of us more productive.'

Barnaby smiled inscrutably. 'I'm not familiar with these journals myself. Q1?'

'A mix.'

'We need to aim for Q1, Ash. Have a look at the email circulated last week by the research office.'

Ashraf cleared his throat, but Barnaby pressed on.

'Student feedback forms are average.' He squinted as he studied a page closely. 'A dip in your ratings last semester.'

'Coinciding with an increase in the word counts of the assessments,' Ashraf said. He was getting flustered.

'Look, are you trying to say that I'm still not competitive for promotion?'

Barnaby shuffled the papers back into a neat pile on his desk and sat up straight. 'Ash, what value would you say you're adding to our department?'

Ashraf opened his mouth to answer, but Barnaby raised his hand silently. He was not done.

Ashraf sank back in his chair.

'By "value" I mean *big-picture* value. Your scholarly output is important, nobody can deny that. But we want to be change-makers. We're living in an increasingly destructive, dehumanising global social and political order, Ash.'

Ashraf blinked, confused. Barnaby lived in a property in Edgecliff with a water view and was married to the CFO of a hedge fund.

'If we aren't working on the most urgent dilemmas of our time,' he continued, without a trace of irony, 'then other universities will seize the opportunities that people like you deserve.'

'People like me?'

Barnaby explained that he was fed up with the way institutions used diversity as window dressing instead of valuing the decolonial, alternative knowledge and perspectives of scholars of colour.

'*Decolonisation is not just a metaphor*, Ash,' he said passionately. '*You* aren't just a metaphor, a statistic in our annual diversity report. You have a rich heritage, unique networks and connections. You need to find a way to tap into that, prove that our diverse JBU community here is not cynical tokenism but meaningful on its own terms.'

'I wasn't aware I was a token.'

'I don't believe you are,' Barnaby said quietly but firmly. 'But, at this underwhelming pace, you aren't doing much to disprove those who might make that undue assumption and pass you over for bigger opportunities.'

Barnaby stood up, abruptly signalling the end of the review. 'Let's schedule a follow-up meeting next month to give you time to work on pursuing new projects, collaborations and grant opportunities. We'll touch base then to see what you can deliver.'

Barnaby sat back down. 'My door is always open if you need any advice,' he said. 'But, please, close it on your way out to keep the aircon in.'

Feeling dazed and off kilter, Ashraf tapped his ID card on the photocopy machine and released his PhD student Jamal's latest draft chapters for printing. He'd decided to head home early. Not only was he exhausted from taking the first flight out of Melbourne to make it to campus in time for his performance review, but he also now felt the unsettling weight of having to prove himself. Again.

It had been a relief when Jamal had cancelled their meeting, saying his baby had been unwell and that he needed a bit more time to catch up on his research before their meeting. Ashraf didn't have the headspace for mentoring today. He would read Jamal's chapters after marking a pile of essays on 'TikTok and human rights' from the comfort of his home instead.

Aside from a small group of higher degree research students huddled around one table, the communal lounge area was empty. He crossed the room and sat down in a deceptively hard, bright-orange sofa to wait for his printing as far as possible from the students, took out his phone and found an ABC News alert. Following the link to a video, he recognised the interviewee's face: Leena, a Palestinian academic from New South Wales University of Technology.

'Palestinians are rising up against Israel in a unity intifada – meaning *uprising*,' she explained to the blonde, blue-eyed anchor.

The anchor leant forward in his swivel chair, animated, indignant, primed for this moment. '*Intifada*?'

The interview was a train wreck. While Ashraf sympathised with Leena having to answer the usual *do you condemn* questions, he was disappointed that she hadn't taken the opportunity to speak to her audience on their terms. The ABC audience wanted something they could sigh about at the water cooler; they weren't interested in Leena lecturing them about settler colonialism and racism.

It was like this whenever a Palestinian advocate was interviewed. They displayed remarkable naivety in presuming that audiences were interested in Balfour or Oslo when – and he could be confident, given the number of students he'd taught in his academic career – most people didn't even know the history or politics of this country, let alone know or care for the history and political machinations of another.

As if operating with such delusion was not bad enough, these advocates and spokespeople also tended to present as always angry, rigid and uncompromising, thus reinforcing the very stereotypes that prevented people from sympathising with them. They missed the precious opportunity to use the time and platform they were so rarely afforded to get people on their side.

Leena was a classic case in point. She was defensive, her responses were inflected with aggression ('Why are you asking me how settlers feel?') and she was being dangerously intransigent in her refusal to condemn Palestinian violence.

Even though the violence was retaliatory – yes, he knew that as an Arab and as somebody who had read more books on Israel and Palestine in one week than this news anchor probably had in his lifetime – Ashraf also knew that nobody, least of all the mainstream media and its consumers, were interested in causes over effects. Leena had well and truly messed up by insisting on historical context and structural explanations instead of presenting the only thing that might move a middle-aged white audience: trauma.

The photocopy machine beeped loudly to signal the finished job, so he got up, grabbed the chapters and stuffed them in his satchel. Not wanting to get stuck with the crowd of students getting into the lift, Ashraf hung back a bit and refreshed his Twitter feed. Right at the top was a Channel 5 TV News video about Al-Bayinnah. He tapped the thumbnail and turned up the volume when he saw his sister-in-law, Fayza, in a striking olive-green suit and maroon-and-purple hijab, on screen.

Fayza was trying to dodge a blonde reporter in an electric-blue suit, flanked by a cameraman, who was shoving a microphone in her face. Fayza sidestepped them both and strode to her car looking tense yet dignified.

The reporter, in a breathless, urgent tone, ended the story looking directly into the camera. 'Al-Bayinnah's principal, Fayza Sayid, insists she and her school have nothing to hide and yet still refuses to speak to the media. Parents, neighbours and the public have many unanswered questions. The most pressing of them: is Al-Bayinnah a school of students or a school of terrorists?'

Ashraf didn't believe in private schools, least of all religious independent schools. And definitely not Islamic schools. It was a position he'd held consistently, though perhaps more dogmatically after Mya decided to leave the land of the infidels.

Before meeting Abdel-Karim, but after her religious awakening, Mya had spent months proselytising to Ashraf. She begged him to practise the faith, observe the rituals. He understood why she needed him to. Everything that they shared in common, which had sustained their relationship until then, she now designated as haram – and her new legislation was retrospective.

She'd started talking about migrating to a Muslim country. 'How do we raise our girls here, in this hyper-sexualised, hyper-consumerist society that worships me-culture and materialism?' she'd asked.

'There's a shopping mall in the clocktower in Mecca,' Ashraf had replied.

Mya conceded the point. It would therefore be better to live outside the cities, she'd argued, in a place where 'we can authentically practise our values'.

In desperation, he'd offered a compromise. They could enrol the girls in Al-Bayinnah, under the guidance of Mya's own sister, Fayza. A little Muslim island in a sea of infidels. Would that make her happy?

It hadn't. Mya loved and admired her sister's efforts, but she told him, 'The system is bigger than Fayza.' She had no interest in socialising their daughters in the 'whitewashing multicultural liberal agenda' of Islamic schools that, 'ironically, cosy up to the white thieving Australian colony for their funding, ignoring the fact they're on stolen land'.

He remembered Fayza calling him after Mya had announced to the family that she would be moving to Yemen with her new husband and the girls.

'I tried to persuade her to stay and for the girls to attend my school,' Fayza had told Ashraf. 'But she flatly refused.'

Mya's refusal had wounded Fayza deeply. That wound was, no matter that they were no longer in regular touch, an enduring bond between Ashraf and Fayza. It was for this reason that Ashraf decided to send Fayza a text message: *I saw the news. Are you okay?*

The lift pinged open again, mercifully empty, and she replied before he'd even had a chance to hit the button for B2. A few texts were exchanged, Ramadan Kareem et cetera. By the time Ashraf reached his car, Fayza had invited him to join her family for iftar on Saturday night.

The scent of eucalyptus and an ocean breeze candle hit him as soon as he opened the front door to his unit. Ashraf had forgotten the cleaner, Chantelle, was there.

Not wanting to startle her he called out her name, but there was no response – only the sound of somebody moving around in the kitchen. He crossed the living space, and approached the door to the kitchen, calling her name again as he turned on the air-conditioning. His apartment, encased in large floor-to-ceiling windows, overheated easily.

With her AirPods in her ears, Chantelle was oblivious to his return. She wore faded black leggings, a bleach-stained t-shirt and green plastic flip-flops. He had no choice but to plant himself in front of her and announce his presence. She let out a small scream, then, realising it was him, placed one hand on her chest and fanned her face with the other.

Ashraf apologised.

Chantelle smiled and nodded. Her face was flushed red from cleaning in stuffy, greenhouse conditions.

'Why didn't you turn on the AC?' he asked.

She looked at him blankly. He had found her via Airtasker. She was on a student visa from China, studying business at uni. The syntax and grammar of her messages on Airtasker had been flawless. In person, she barely spoke English and didn't understand his instructions. He hadn't intended to hire her again, but she sent him a sequence of word-perfect messages imploring him to keep her on. Her university fees were exorbitant, her rent was high and she needed the money. He succumbed.

He pointed to the air-conditioning panel on the wall and attempted some gestures. She nodded again, half laughed and then turned around to continue doing the dishes. He didn't consider it appropriate to be in the apartment while Chantelle was working as he felt his presence probably made her feel uncomfortable, so he grabbed a beer from the fridge, a couple of apples and his laptop, and ventured out onto the balcony overlooking the velvety green panorama of Kensington Golf Club. He was grateful there was a breeze. He would drink his beer, mark essays and, most importantly, distract himself from the two overwhelming questions that had just been presented to him: namely, whether his job was in jeopardy and just what the hell kind of new project he was going to come up with.

He started marking essays online, according to the rubric he was sure most students hadn't bothered to look at. He had always been conscientious (*Does that count as a value-add, Barnaby?*), but he couldn't offer the detailed feedback he would have liked because a consultant with no pedagogical training had determined academics should mark five essays per hour and Barnaby had sent an all-staff email reminder that there would be no overtime paid.

A few hours later, Chantelle paid and gone, apples demolished, essays marked and bell-curved, he slammed his laptop shut. He lay back in the deckchair, closed his eyes and thought about academics he could potentially invite to collaborate with him on a project. But then that didn't make much sense given he had no project with which to entice them.

Maybe he could just think of a past successful project and add 'decolonial' to it. Or maybe he could do a project drawn from his own life: 'From Sydney to Aden: How modern Muslim women are giving up feminism'. Surely grant money would be thrown at that.

8

On the weekend Hannah and Jamal's network of Muslim friends, and the fifteen children between them, gathered at the Newington Community Centre.

By the time Hannah arrived with Jamal and Aya, Nahla, informally designated as the event planner due to her impeccable organisational skills in a group beset by a chronic inability to make decisions, had been at the hall for a few hours already to set up. She'd draped a Palestine flag and a 'Ramadan Mubarak' banner over the blinds behind a long table weighed down with an eclectic spread of dishes.

The vapers huddled in the back courtyard, taking their first drags since sunrise. A few of the older girls balanced their phones on a windowsill and recorded TikTok videos. Hind's mother-in-law – exiled from Sudan and now dividing her life between her children in Sydney, Oman and Norway – sat on a rattan outdoor chair that was too big for her and gripped a cup of Arabic coffee as she watched the girls with a smile on her face. The younger kids played soccer on the back grass area, using two large eskies as goalposts, ignoring the warnings of the vaping adults to kick low so the ball didn't go over the fence and onto the road. Aya was in a cheeky mood, playing peekaboo with Dana and Rida.

Hannah smiled, soaking up the rhythm of the iftar, which hummed along to the cadence of 'We teach life, sir'. She took a seat inside at one of several round tables arranged for dining, next to some of her friends, everyone talking over each other, sharing their most exasperating Facebook Marketplace negotiation stories.

'I listed it for free,' Jasmine said, 'and the guy still had the audacity to ask me to deliver it to him.'

'No,' Rida said. 'The worst are the ones who come in a Kia to pick up an eight-seater dining table and then act surprised when it doesn't fit.'

The conversation then pivoted to whether Mark Ruffalo, who had been tweeting about Palestine, was legit or a grifter. Then it turned to swapping banoffee pie recipe notes, and that somehow led to Jasmine taking out her phone to show them all a video of police raiding Nabil's house, which then led to a heated fight about whether he was a hero or a victim.

'It was stupid and naive of him,' Jasmine said. 'He basically delivered a perfect gift to the Israel lobby.'

'He's only a kid,' Ari argued. 'You can't blame him. There are literal neo-Nazis streaming live and nothing happens.'

'It doesn't matter. Hamas is listed as illegal. He should've known better.'

'He's only eighteen,' Hannah said impatiently. 'Cut him some slack.'

'Well, nobody's talking about why they were protesting now, are they?' Jasmine said. 'It's a total distraction! But you're right, he's only a kid. It's not fair. Those Aussie activists at JBU weren't carrying the flag and they were uni students, older. Why didn't they tell him?' She paused, eyes wide. 'I bet they set him up. There are infiltrators, you know.'

Zara, dressed in an all-white jumpsuit, gold hoop earrings and impossibly high heels, suddenly appeared, shoving Hannah and Ari apart to squeeze her chair in between them. 'One more minute with Basil and Soha and I'm going to scream,' she hissed. 'They're *so* pushy. It's nobody's business if I vaccinate Mona.'

Nabil and infiltrators were forgotten and Hannah found herself caught up in an argument with Zara, who had a two-year-old daughter, ran a real estate agency in St Leonards and voted Liberal.

'You too?' Zara rolled her eyes. 'It's an industry. It's all about profiting the pharmaceutical industry, okay? They're invested in keeping us all unwell. And we just don't know what's in them.'

'Babe,' Hannah said playfully. 'You vape.'

'So?' Zara was undeterred. 'Every second person today is neurodivergent this and autistic that. You can't convince me it's not because of the chemicals pumped into our bodies.'

'You've got filler in your face and don't tell me that's just lip plumper.'

'Stop being so judgemental,' Zara said.

'I'm not!' Hannah protested. 'You look great. But at least have a consistent argument. I swear I don't know how we're still friends.'

Zara tilted her head to the side and flashed a brilliant smile. 'For over two decades now, babe.'

Hannah and Zara had been family friends since they were kids, forced to go to Arabic school together along with Nahla and Hind. She was one of those friends who Hannah caught up with a few times a year in these big gatherings and that was more than enough.

Zara fiddled with an earring. 'Anyway, I'm not going to risk my child's body. Oh hey!' Zara suddenly lurched forward and grabbed Hannah's wrist. 'There's a flat in my building up for lease. I know the landlord. I'll make sure you're looked after. You and Jamal need to upgrade. Get out of Western Sydney. We can be neighbours!'

'No thanks. I'm very happy with the gangs, bad roads and five-dollar mana'eesh.'

'So you *do* get it,' Zara said.

Jamal, who had been in conversation with Basil and Soha, appeared behind Hannah and started massaging her shoulders.

'Jamal,' Zara ordered, 'talk some sense into Hannah.'

'Oh?'

'You really must move across the bridge. I've got an apartment that's perfect for you guys.'

'The Australian visa was hard enough, Zara. I think immigration to Sydney's North Shore might be even harder.'

'I'm serious,' Zara said. 'It's not a safe place to raise kids.'

Jamal leant over Hannah and reached for a piece of fruit from her plate.

'You forget where I was born and raised,' he said to Zara. 'I come from everyday Armageddon.' He popped a grape into his mouth.

'Hm?'

'Suheir Hammad,' he said, the half-chewed grape slightly muffling his words.

'Hm?'

'His favourite poet,' Hannah explained.

'The rent is very reasonable,' Zara said, and then turned to speak to Ari.

Jamal squeezed Hannah's shoulder affectionately, bid them all salams, and walked over to a table set up for tea and coffee.

Hannah took a bite out of her caramel slice, Gada's speciality and a staple at every iftar gathering, and sat in her thoughts as she chewed slowly, watching Aya across the room still being cuddled by Dana and Rida.

They were all constantly encountering their lives through a lenticular lens. Viewed from one angle: joy, love, laughter, tensions, privilege, routine. Viewed from the slightest tilt: tragedy, injustice, oppression.

She recalled an inspirational quote that had shown up on her Insta feed the day before in a Lexend font on a green tile: *You're not healing to handle the trauma. You know how to do that. You're healing to handle the joy.* Cheesy, but it resonated.

She truly struggled at handling joy *here* as Nakba continued *there*. She wrestled with the temptation to despair. It felt self-indulgent, a luxury. She had too much self-respect to capitulate.

Hannah stood swiftly, marched outside to the children still playing soccer and cajoled them into posing for a big, crazy group photo.

9

He arrived five minutes past iftar. Hasan, Fayza's Malaysian-born husband, embraced Ashraf in a long hug at the door and handed him a date and a glass of water before leading him down the hallway towards the backyard.

'I wasn't fasting, but I love dates,' Ashraf said, and popped the date into his mouth.

Hasan smiled, seemingly without judgement, and ushered Ashraf outside into the pergola. A red, yellow, white and blue Ramadan Khayamiya tablecloth covered an eight-seater, decorated with Ramadan kitsch he'd seen in Facebook Etsy ads: lanterns, a white bejewelled crescent moon stand, a wooden mosque. Hasan invited Ashraf to take a seat.

The pergola was large but cluttered. Ashraf stepped around sporting equipment lying against an exercise bike and dodged a hanging fake pot plant. Two hookahs were balanced on top of a large grey outdoor chest, which was squashed close to a white-wicker egg chair in one corner. The pergola overlooked a pool running adjacent to a fading white concrete wall that separated the house from the Hume Highway on the other side. It was meant to be a noise barrier, but Ashraf could still make out the traffic.

Hasan poured him a glass of fresh lemon and mint juice.

'How's Fayza holding up?' Ashraf asked.

'She's doing just fine,' Fayza replied for Hasan as she stepped outside to join them. She sat down across from Ashraf, beside her husband.

Seeing Fayza in person, Ashraf was reminded of how little resemblance Fayza and Mya bore to each other. Fayza resembled his ex-mother-in-law: dark prominent eyebrows arched over large, protruding dark-brown eyes, thick brown lips and a brown complexion. Mya took after their half-Egyptian, half-Turkish father: light skin prone to burning, not tanning, light-brown eyes and a thinner mouth. Fayza wore her hijab in colourful scarves and twisted turbans. Mya had gone from having cascading curly hair to wearing plain, dark-coloured scarves pinned tightly under her chin, the material dangling loose over her chest.

'It's not my welfare that's of concern here,' Fayza said in her characteristically no-nonsense tone after they'd gone through the small talk and settled down to eat.

Fayza had, to Ashraf's delight, made a suite of dishes including koshari. It had been a while since he'd eaten a decent Egyptian dish – and not because he wasn't capable of making one. Mya had loathed cooking as much as Ashraf had loved it, which was a good arrangement when he had a family to cook for. It was hard to muster the motivation to cook for an empty table.

'I have six hundred students who are being used by politicians for their own agendas, and harassed by the media. And let's not forget that all the attention is on Nabil when the other protesters were also arrested.'

'Yes, well, maybe that's because he was holding a Hamas flag,' Ashraf said. 'And banging on about armed resistance.'

Fayza was clearly frustrated. 'You know very well it's all just politics.'

The sliding door opened. It was Youmna, Fayza's daughter, who beamed when she saw Ashraf. The last time Ashraf had seen Youmna was just after the divorce. She was his girls' closest cousin, just a few months younger than Shaymaa. Although his daughters – who had grown up in the eastern suburbs – and Youmna – who had grown up in the southwest – didn't attend the same school or live near each other, they'd all spent countless weekends, picnics, getaways and holidays together.

Youmna vigorously shook Ashraf's hand. 'It's been ages, Amo Ashraf.' Her eyes landed on the spread of food and she plopped down in a chair, adjusted her hijab, which had slipped back slightly, and started helping herself to koshari with lashings of chilli sauce.

'Did you finish your assessment?' Fayza asked.

Ashraf watched as Youmna eyeballed her mother and said, through a mouth full of food, 'Mum! Get off my back, will you?'

Still, Fayza tried to pep-talk Youmna, deploying scripts she had clearly rehearsed on students at her school.

Youmna made no effort to conceal her boredom and turned to face Ashraf. 'So, what brings you here?'

Ashraf smiled. 'I wanted to check in after I saw the news.'

Youmna sat up straighter, animated. 'On Friday morning one of the news channels was waiting for us in the street that leads up to the school's back gate.'

Hasan tutted.

'They were yelling out at us, trying to bait us.'

'Don't give them even one—'

'Yes, Mum – I'm not an idiot, I *know*! Fetu and Moey from next door yelled at them to back off.'

Fayza's eyebrows shot up. 'From the car repairs?'

'Yeah,' Youmna said, grinning.

'How do you know their names?'

'Because they're hot.' Youmna burst out laughing, thoroughly enjoying riling her mother up.

'MashAllah,' Hasan said, rolling his eyes. 'Islamic school education, Ashraf.'

'Relax, Taliban,' Youmna said to her parents. 'Anyway, Fetu and Moey weren't that convincing because the journalists didn't back off. So we bolted down the street and snuck in through another gate before they had a chance to catch up.'

Fayza's eyes flashed angrily. 'They're trying so hard to get to the students. The police are too.'

Youmna scraped her chair closer to the table, whipped out her phone and leant in. 'Check this out: "Nobody plans a terrorist attack alone", "Shut down the school and make them talk". Here's a petition to shut down all Islamic schools. It's got' – she brought the phone closer to her face – 'three thousand signatures. Here's another petition called "We Pay Fees for Maths Not Jihad in Schools" that wants Mum to be sacked as principal, started by some sellout called "Mohammed A Concerned Parent", and another one calling for Nabil to be sent back to Lebanon even though he was born in Australia, scumbags!'

Fayza took a deep calming breath. 'You need to ignore the media. I want you to focus on your exams and leave me to worry about all this.'

'You expect me to switch off and go back to writing essays on *Jane Austen* when Nabil was swapping assessment notes with me a couple of weeks ago?'

Ashraf could sense a mother/principal–daughter/student stand-off.

Fayza and Youmna stared at each other, tense and combative.

Ashraf decided to jump in before either had a chance to engage. 'Did he show any signs?' he asked. 'Weren't there any clues?'

Fayza sighed. 'Signs? Of what?'

'You can't deny the fact he was holding a Hamas flag, Fayza,' Ashraf said.

'Does that make him Hamas's recruitment manager?'

'You're being naive,' Ashraf said with surprise. 'And flippant. This is a potential terrorism case.'

'Obviously I understand the gravity,' Fayza said. 'And what I tell my students and staff is very different from what I can say here.'

'And you had no idea?' Ashraf asked.

'He's been a student with us since Year 5. One of our more boisterous boys. Teachers either loved him or clashed with him. He was in my office at least once a month – either sent to me from class in trouble or there on his own accord to chat about my day, ask me how I was.'

There was no mistaking the affection in her tone.

'Paul Kram is the only teacher who's come out and said he isn't surprised, but knowing Paul he's just trying to gain clout in the staffroom.'

Ashraf perked up. 'What do you mean?'

'He brought up a history essay Nabil wrote last term. Apparently, it was about freeing Muslim lands from the West.'

Ashraf raised an eyebrow at Fayza. 'There you go,' he said, almost triumphantly.

'Oh, please. I'm not going to make that kind of ridiculous leap,' Fayza snapped.

'I mean, he could be an obnoxious idiot one minute and the nicest guy the next,' Youmna added. 'In other words, like most guys in my orbit.'

'I'm sorry to labour the point but I just don't understand how there were no other warning signs,' Ashraf insisted. 'There are patterns, signs. It doesn't just happen overnight. It's gradual and slow at first and then suddenly you can't *not* notice it.' Ashraf felt himself getting a little too worked up for his liking. He paused, took a deep breath.

Fayza watched him intently, knowingly.

'That's what the media says,' Hasan said. 'That Fayza and the teachers should have picked it up.'

'Bro, you're making it sound like he had a virus,' Youmna said.

Hasan turned to Ashraf. 'She calls me bro.'

'Dude saw Palestinians being killed and caged and was angry. And the entire world watches on so no shit Hamas steps in because the UN is useless.'

'Youmna, I don't want to hear you talking like that,' Fayza said angrily.

'Mum, I'm not stupid. I'm just stating facts. If they, like, don't want Hamas, don't give Hamas a reason to exist.'

'I don't even want to hear you talking that way to *us*,' Fayza said. 'It's too risky.'

Youmna gave her a blistering look. 'So much for *Youmna get off TikTok and use your brain*.'

'Look,' Ashraf said, trying to defuse the situation, 'this all just proves that we need to find constructive ways for young people to channel anger.'

Youmna rolled her eyes. 'Won't somebody save the youth.'

Fayza folded her arms across her chest and rubbed her elbows. 'I agree, Ashraf. But it doesn't make this witch-hunt any easier to accept. We're there to teach students, not treat every teenage rant as a crime. You asked me if there were signs. Look, all the teachers are shocked. Not that Nabil would participate in a protest but that he would do something so reckless.'

Fazya stood up, indicating that part of the conversation was over.

'Let's have dessert and coffee,' she said, 'and move on to less controversial topics, like how we can mobilise Islamic schools to have strong student and teacher contingents at climate change rallies.' She gathered some plates and headed inside.

'And that's my cue,' Youmna said and rose from the table. She left calling out 'Bye!' as she escaped the threat of another boring conversation.

'Come on,' Hasan said, also rising from the table. 'Let's have coffee inside.'

'Your wife preaches about climate change,' Ashraf said drolly. 'My wife's preaching was about how my Spotify account will land me in hell.'

'I guess a different kind of climate change,' Hasan said with a grin.

10

Hannah woke up to Aya's crying and rushed to the nursery. When cuddles, rocking and patting wouldn't settle her, Hannah returned to her bedroom with Aya, propped herself up in bed and put Aya on her breast. She picked up her phone from the bedside table and saw a WhatsApp notification in Arabic from Jamal's mother Warda in the family group chat: 'Ya Allah, pray for our safety, ya habaayib. They're bombing.'

Hannah reached over to Jamal to wake him up, but the jerky movement dislodged her breast from Aya's mouth. Aya let out a cry and Hannah quickly put her back on.

'Jamal!'

It took a few seconds for Jamal to stir, and to register Hannah's tone and then also her words: 'They're bombing Gaza!' He bolted upright.

Hannah showed Jamal the message.

He grabbed his phone and called his mother.

The call rang out.

He tried again. And again. And again.

'Ya Allah!' he kept repeating, pacing the room and reading the news on his phone as Hannah, tied to Aya and unable to physically console him, tried offering words of consolation.

They were both consumed by their phones, digesting every piece of news, every tweet, every social media update.

One mother tweeted: *Tonight we will all sleep together in the one room. If we die, at least we will be martyred together and nobody will be forced to live alone in grief.*

Finally, Aya drifted off to sleep and had dislodged from Hannah's chest. Hannah looked down at her tiny button nose, long black eyelashes, cherub cheeks and, overcome with a wave of nausea – seeing every baby in Gaza in Aya's face – she raised Aya close to her face, needing to hear her breathe. Here she was with her baby, breathing, safe, in Merrylands, not Al Jabalia. She was here in the diaspora of their murderous empire, an exile, racked with survivor's guilt, numbed with survivor's relief.

The images, the images, the images.

She started to sob silently while Jamal kept trying to reach his mother.

It was almost time for suhoor when Jamal finally connected with Warda by text message. She was still alive. That was the update. For now.

Even though Jamal told her it would be impossible to speak on the phone, impossible to hear anything through the roar of F-15s pounding the tiny strip of land, he tried calling his relatives one by one, hoping in vain that somebody would pick up and he'd hear a voice. He eventually gave up trying to call and settled for a stream of text message updates for confirmation of life.

Jamal told Hannah that his sister, Tasnim, was hiding her small children Farha and Zaid under the kitchen sink. She sat beside the kitchen sink cupboard alone – Israeli forces had shot and killed her husband, Nader, in the Great March of Return three years ago – and tried to distract her daughter and son, reciting Quranic verses with them even though their voices were drowned out by the roar of planes and drones.

'Bastards!' Hannah said through gritted teeth. She decided it was time to put Aya back in her cot. Once Aya was down, Hannah shut the door quietly, joined Jamal in the kitchen and turned on the baby monitor.

Jamal moved through the suhoor preparations differently to Hannah. He was tense, stiff, quiet.

He had grown up in Gaza. He was thirteen when Israel imposed the blockade. He was fourteen when he survived Israel's 2008 war on Gaza. He was eighteen when his baby sister was diagnosed with a hole in her heart and Israel refused to grant her a travel permit for treatment in Jerusalem and so she died. He was twenty when he survived Israel's next war on Gaza. He was twenty-one when he left Gaza for Australia, leaving his family behind. He was twenty-four when his family and friends marched in the Great March of Return. And he was still twenty-four when his brother-in-law Nader was shot in the head by an Israeli sniper, when his best friend Emad – the sore loser at card games, the one who would give you the shirt off his back – was shot in the back and paralysed, when Issa – his tutor at Gaza University – was shot in the ankle and disabled.

Hannah knew that Jamal had learnt to compartmentalise his rage and grief, had learnt a level of self-restraint that can perhaps only come from living through slow-cooked trauma.

Hannah, on the other hand, swore and yelled. She felt like a vessel perched under an open tap, rage gushing over her and overflowing the rim. There was no pause, no moment of hollow, empty, luxurious nothingness. Just rage cascading over rage. She refused to catch or contain it. She let it pour out.

She had observed this when they went to Palestine together for their honeymoon (which they started in Bali and ended in the homeland). At Allenby, at the checkpoints, in restaurants in Jaffa and Jerusalem, Jamal constantly had to restrain Hannah and calm her down.

Now they worked in rhythm in the kitchen. Cooking was, Hannah felt, a way to put her rage in order. She diced cucumbers, sliced through the thickness of pain and anger. They listened to *Al Jazeera* live on Hannah's phone, which she propped up against a chipped Luna Park mug. Jamal fried eggs, Hannah prepared a dish of oil and zaatar, and Gaza burnt under Israeli airstrikes.

Then they sat at the kitchen island, eating slowly, watching the news, punctuating the rolling coverage of Israeli airstrikes with duas and 'Can you pass the bread?' and 'Jamal, you have to help me stop swearing. It's Ramadan, for God's sake.'

They prayed fajr together and then curled up in bed and fell asleep.

11

Ashraf was waiting for the lift to travel up from the lower levels of the car park when he heard someone sing out 'Marhaba ya zalamee!' – the hometown-Yorkie accent unblunted by Duolingo.

Ashraf turned to see Brendan smiling broadly and walking towards him. He forced himself to return the upbeat greeting.

There was no avoiding Brendan, or his habit of practising his Arabic whenever he saw him. He was, Ashraf had to begrudgingly admit, an affable colleague. It was a compliment precisely because of Brendan's prodigious academic track record. In Ashraf's experience, warmth was rarely concomitant with academic superstardom.

When the doors to the lift opened, a man wearing a dress, Dr Martens, pearl earrings and pink nail polish shifted to the side to make room for Ashraf and Brendan to enter.

Ashraf nodded his thanks but couldn't help tensing up. He heard Brendan cough awkwardly and noticed, in his peripheral vision, that he was fiddling with his novelty golf bag cufflinks.

The lift stopped at the ground floor and the man – Ashraf wondered if he was supposed to call him a woman – stepped off.

'I'm all for live and let live,' Brendan said when they were alone, 'but *really*.'

Ashraf raised his eyebrows to signal agreement but did not trust Brendan enough to be too profuse about it. The world had, as far as Ashraf was concerned, gone mad. Between these trans freaks on the one hand and the religious freaks on the other, there was nothing the world of wokeness needed more than a Goddamn dose of melatonin. He didn't know where he fit in.

As the lift slowly made its way up to level 6, Brendan started telling Ashraf about a multi-regional four-year project funded by the EU that he had just been added to. 'We're looking at democratic governance, and digital and green futures as a multilateral comparative study.'

'Sounds urgent and important,' Ashraf managed, relieved that the lift had arrived at his floor. 'Congratulations.'

'And what about you?' Brendan said from inside the lift, as Ashraf exited. 'What are you working on at the moment?'

'Um, the Arab World.'

'Fascinating.' Brendan smiled at Ashraf as the doors closed.

Ashraf walked to his office feeling deflated. He dropped his satchel next to his desk and sank into his chair.

His phone vibrated. He fished it out of his pocket to find a new email.

Dear Dr Magdy,

My name is Simon Chester and I'm with the Department of Home Affairs' National Commission on Fostering Social Cohesion and Harmony.

I attended your panel at the Melbourne conference last week and was very impressed. With your outstanding academic credentials, lived experience, intimate understanding of the Middle East and your Islamic background, we believe you would make an invaluable contribution to our new expert taskforce.

I would be pleased if you would contact me at your earliest convenience to set up a meeting to discuss this further.

I look forward to hearing from you.

Warm regards,
Simon Chester

Ashraf's heart was racing. He tried to focus on his breathing to calm his body down.

He'd had so few celebrations lately, so few reasons to feel seen, worthy, motivated.

Finally, some good news. It was about time.

Though Simon was now working in the public service, he'd had, he assured Ashraf over Zoom a few hours later, a long and, he was proud to say, rigorous academic career built on working with marginalised, mainly Arab and Muslim, male youth communities.

'I spent years researching the role of cultures of masculinity in violent extremism and terrorism – and the attraction of men especially to jihadist ideologies,' Simon told him.

Ashraf studied the pristine and purposely arranged bookshelf behind Simon. His large frame was flanked by a collection that ranged from Edward Said to Noam Chomsky to Jordan Peterson.

'We've looked closely at your body of work, Ashraf,' Simon said.

'You can call me Ash.'

'Oh, okay, well, as I said in my email, we're very impressed. Your work on transnational activism in the Middle East is particularly appealing to our CVE – countering violent extremism – projects. We don't want to stop people exercising their right to protest. We're here to find ways to ensure it doesn't impact social cohesion.'

There was a delicate line between being eager and appearing desperate, so Ashraf, trying hard to contain his excitement, asked some questions to at least seem to be contemplating the merits of the role. Truly, he just wanted to know how soon he could start.

'How do you see my role in the team?' he asked. 'Will I be working on extremism as it pertains to Arab and Muslim communities only, or is there scope to also examine the rise of the far-right and radical leftist activist movements?' and, 'Am I working towards a public-facing report, academic article or policy paper?'

'Each of those questions is a research field in itself,' Simon said. He unbuttoned the cuffs of his shirt, rolling up the sleeves, revealing a tattoo on each forearm: 'appear as you are' on the left arm, 'appear as you be' on the right. Ashraf noticed that part of the tattoo was in Persian script. He deciphered a و and a ر, which was all he needed to conclude that the Persian script spelt out Rumi.

'We know CVE and maintaining social cohesion is a top priority of governments and communities. We're in a dynamic and evolving environment,' Simon said, his tone impassioned. 'Terrorists and extremist groups constantly adapt their methods and we need to ensure our knowledge, capabilities and responses are fit for purpose.'

'Yes, of course,' Ashraf said, nodding along.

'We'd like you to establish a pilot Youth Power project with vulnerable youth, skewed towards Muslim males, empowering them in their identity and political expression.'

'Excellent,' Ashraf said.

He'd done a few projects with students at a community centre in South Western Sydney around the time of the Arab Spring and then the Syrian Uprising, looking at transnational influences in protest chants, motifs and symbols. Granted, the students were more interested in getting out of school and the free food, but he had collected enough data to write up a solid journal paper.

He could do this. He was excited.

'We're seeing tensions again with the Israel–Palestine conflict,' Simon said, 'and we need to be mindful of ways for anger to be channelled constructively.'

Simon then went on to explain the expected outcomes and outline logistics. Ashraf would have a pool of funding, a research associate seconded from the department who would be working from Canberra but available to do tasks online.

Ashraf felt energised, overcome with a sense of purpose and overwhelming relief that he had been given a direction in which to finally point the needle of his career.

He would be expected to produce a public-facing report. He was at liberty to be creative in how he would work with the students, and to take advantage of the possibilities of digital publics and technologies.

He forced himself to focus on maintaining a professional demeanour, took notes to keep his hands busy. While Simon continued to speak, Ashraf's mind raced. Among his thoughts: Barnaby's reaction (approached by the government and handed a pool of funding!), who would be on his team (Jamal had excellent community networks) and what this would mean for his prospects of promotion (only good things, *surely*).

12

Aya had been a fussy, sooky nightmare that morning and without Jamal, who had left home early to teach a class, Hannah was left to deal with Aya and drop her to her mum's on her way to work.

By the time she got to the bus stop, all the closest parking spots were taken. It took several laps before she finally found a three-hour space five streets away between a grey-rendered McMansion and a prefab house. It was a huge risk, but she had no choice. She jumped out of her car under the watch of an elderly lady sitting on a white plastic chair on the front porch of the prefab house.

The lady sucked on a cigarette before yelling in a heavy accent, 'Zay colour za tyres. Make sure you back in time.'

'Thank you!' Hannah called back, although the information was redundant. There would be no time to move the car. She would have to wear the fine.

She ran down Sherwood Road towards the bus stop, regretting her choice of sexy bra over sensible sports bra. She passed the mana'eesh shop, trying her best not to inhale the aroma of fresh dough and zaatar, the movie rental–mixed goods store everybody suspected was a money laundering operation, and That Coffee Shop with its delectable display of ricotta cannoli, gourmet muffins and Campos coffee.

She made it just as the last of the waiting passengers were getting on the bus. Breathless, she scanned her Opal card and found a spot towards the back.

During the bus ride, Hannah listened to the latest updates on the lynching of a Palestinian man in a Tel Aviv suburb by a mob of Israelis; wrestled with forms on myGov; advised a Palestinian-Iraqi lawyer in one of her advocacy WhatsApp groups on whether to push back against four rejections of his op-ed; suggested some edits on a Black–Palestinian solidarity statement; and placed a Coles home delivery order for later that evening, as she'd forgotten to buy nappies last night when she'd gone to Coles solely for the purpose of buying nappies and returned with a trolley full of everything but nappies.

She was a shrivelled prune today, multitasking trauma and banality in a state of disassociation – and thank God for it. Every last tear had poured out of her and onto her prayer mat the night before during qiyam al-layl. She'd begged God to protect Jamal's family.

Hannah sent a message to Jamal's sister, checking in, then switched back to updating her income details and silently cursing the myGov interface. As the app buffered, she looked out the window and remembered last night at the shops – when she clearly wasn't buying nappies. She'd bumped into Tanya from the gym. She was her regular boxing partner in their combo-fit class.

'Hannah!' Tanya had exclaimed, giving Hannah a wide, genuine smile. 'You've missed three weeks! Where have you been?'

'Gaza,' was Hannah's automatic reply. She didn't have a supermarket-aisle explanation for what it is that people do when their homelands are being bombed and so, quickly, she'd backtracked. 'I mean, Ramadan. I paused my membership.'

Tanya had looked at her blankly.

So Hannah explained: 'But Israel is also bombing Gaza, places where my family is from and—'

'Oh, yes, of course. It's so terrible,' Tanya had interrupted, gently touching Hannah's arm.

She'd been genuine, of this Hannah had no doubt.

'That's why I don't watch the news,' Tanya had added. 'It's too depressing.'

It made sense, Hannah supposed, to ignore the news when you're not the news.

The morning domestic news meeting was like being trapped in a parallel universe, everyone pitching random stories about a bird doing something funny or Sydney's changing party habits.

Hannah sat in silence, staring at a mark on the table. Did they not see the same videos and images on social media? With all their mandatory diversity training – 'How to be an active listener', 'Getting to know the "multi-" in multiculturalism' – did they not realise it was Ramadan, almost Eid, and that that might mean something spectacularly devastating at this time?

John, wrapping up the meeting, looked at Peter. 'Your piece on Hamas is running tomorrow.'

Hannah's mouth went dry. Why hadn't she been asked? At least to consult?

'We really need to find a way into Nabil's inner or outer circle,' John continued. 'With Hamas firing rockets into Israel, Nabil holding that flag changes things. We need someone who will talk. Hannah?'

She swallowed the lump in her throat. 'Hmm?'

'Still nothing?'

She shook her head. He didn't need to know she hadn't even tried. She didn't want to throw Nabil or anybody connected to him to the media wolves.

'That's a shame,' he said pointedly, turning to face the others. 'Okay, so any more pitches?'

'Well, it's almost Eid and Israel's bombing Gaza,' Hannah ventured.

John looked back at her, frowning.

'How about a story with a local Muslim who has family there?' she said cautiously. 'We could also interview someone with family in the West Bank or Israel. There's a massive wave of protests and settler violence against Palestinians.'

Bri and Nathan were nodding with a look of vague sympathy. Peter leant back in his chair, slowly caressing his red stubble. Muna, of Indian descent and the only other brown person in the room, sat still, her face neutral, her eyes avoiding Hannah's.

Stupid cow, Hannah thought. *Fine, keep your head down. I wasn't expecting anything from you.*

Muna was senior to Hannah and had climbed the media ladder via lickspittle ingratiation to the editors and a series of viral stories on 'creeping wokeness in universities and the demise of Western civilisation'.

John coughed. Twice.

Hannah couldn't discern if it was a nervous cough or an irritated epiglottis, but that was a micro-thought process she just had to contend with every time she mentioned Palestine in this room.

'Hmm,' John said thoughtfully.

She imagined him swirling the idea in his head as he would swirl wine in a glass.

'Could you find somebody to talk to?'

Hannah considered saying: 'She's sitting right in front of you,' but held back. She actually wondered if the people she worked with for the past five years even remembered she was Palestinian. It certainly wasn't something she concealed.

Where was your honeymoon? *Palestine.*

Where did you get your Christmas earrings? *Palestine.*

What are you bringing for morning tea? *Konafa, one of the most famous dishes from Palestine.*

The more unapologetic and strident she was, the more her desperation to be seen for who she was and all that it meant was interpreted as her being an intense, out of place, angry Arab woman – and, God forbid, whisper it now, *identity politics.*

She could see it in their faces, their desire for her to leave her identity at home, to keep politics and the God-awful complex mess of the Middle fucking East out of their fifteen-minute morning tea opportunity to enjoy some workplace gossip and a debrief on the latest episode of *Lupin*. (Oh my God, Omar Sy is *so* hot!)

She wished – she would swear to God countless times a day – she could leave it at home, sever the personal from the political, sever the political from her work, but that was impossible. As her homeland burnt under airstrikes, as occupation forces and settlers were on a deadly rampage in the West Bank, she felt every part of her body burning as if she was in those demolished buildings, in those olive groves.

Fine, ignore it all during the cold violence of occupation and siege. But during the hot violence of bombs, wasn't this the time to check in, ask how she was doing? Did bombs not warrant attention? When would business as usual become unusual? What would it take?

Hannah felt like an idiot allowing herself to even contemplate these questions. They required a leap of imagination that was beyond most of her colleagues. It would be asking them to understand that her being *here* was because colonialism was not a one-time event; it was a constant process, a haunting, a forever-shadow, and it weighed on her even as she agreed at their morning teas that Julie's tone to Nathan had, once again, been utterly uncalled for and that Omar Sy was indeed a total babe.

Could you find somebody to talk to? John had asked her.

Like placing a knee on an overpacked suitcase, she shoved her 'identity politics' back inside her, held it all down and forced the zip to close.

'Yes, I can,' she opted to reply. 'For sure.'

John gave her a nod of approval. 'Confine it to a family from Gaza,' he added. 'It's complicated enough. And don't let this interfere with the Nabil story.'

Hannah spent the morning on the phone to Liliana, a nurse in Melbourne whose sister, brother, aunts and uncles were all in the Jabalia camp. Liliana's cousin's family had been killed the night before, leaving Yassin – ten years old – the only survivor.

'He survived,' Liliana explained, 'because his father's body protected him when their building was bombed.'

At the conclusion of the interview Liliana asked Hannah to promise that her story would not be presented alongside an Israeli story, or she would 'decline to proceed'.

Hannah winced. 'I can't promise anything,' she managed, stumbling over her words. 'I wish I could. But I'll speak to my editor. I'll make it clear I support you on this.'

Liliana didn't answer straight away, but eventually she said: 'I trust you will try.'

Hannah worked through lunch, didn't leave her desk until the story was finished. She arranged for a Melbourne photographer to meet Liliana and filed the piece by three with a message she laboured over far longer than it deserved. (She needed to be assertive but not aggressive, deferential but not docile.) She settled on:

Dear John,

Please find attached my piece on the impact of Israel's bombing campaign in Gaza on a Palestinian Australian family.

Please note that Liliana agreed to this interview on the condition that there is no attempt to two-sides her story by presenting an Israeli perspective in the piece. Appreciate if we could respect her wishes.

Thanks,
Hannah

John responded with two lines:

> We're giving this person a 900-word feature with exposure to a national audience. But, noted.

Hannah had no idea what to say. If she pushed back, he might very well take her off the story – and all future stories on Palestine and Israel. He might write her off as a troublemaker, dismiss the subject as being too much of a headache and therefore best avoided altogether. Alternatively, he might decide that being Palestinian, Arab and Muslim meant she was too 'invested' (as he put it to her when she first started in 2018 and had sought to do a story about Gaza's Great March of Return) and that, while the story *should* be covered, it was more suitable in the hands of a neutral (white) journalist.

Hannah decided it was safer to not respond. She was desperate for caffeine, but it would be another two hours and twenty-three minutes before she could down a short black. Head pounding, she went outside and walked a slow lap around the building listening to her favourite Quran recitation through her headphones.

Tired, but not yet ready to return to the office, she sat on a bench in the leafy courtyard, bent forward, elbows resting on her thighs, and scrolled through the news on her phone.

Peter had a new piece, just published online: *Parents Unhappy at Al-Bayinnah.*

Hannah jolted up and read it.

The headline said *parents*, but Peter had only quoted one parent: a Mohamed, no surname, who'd withdrawn his child from Year 10 last year because the school had 'prioritised religion over education', whatever that meant. Mohamed was quoted in the piece as feeling 'certain that there were heaps of parents who were unhappy but were too scared to speak up'.

The article ended with Peter quoting a radicalisation expert from Bond University who offered a few sentences about social cohesion and supporting students in times of crises in the Middle East.

How, Hannah wondered, anger rising within her, *was this a story?*

13

Ashraf got into work at dawn. He scanned his card at the building's glass doors and entered a dark cavernous foyer. It was eerie. It was silent. It had once evoked boredom at best, dread at worst, and yet it was now a promised land, a site of infinite possibilities – within, of course, the parameters of the Youth Power project brief and budget.

The lift opened and he made his way through the newly renovated building and along the central corridor of his department, the bright sensor lights activating section by section, slightly illuminating the books, posters, stickers, folders and personal effects within the offices.

Leigh Carter, upon being appointed as the faculty's research director three months ago, had moved over to this side of the building from the history department. She specialised in the history of rebellions, riots and protests, and she'd quickly made her office, which was next door to his, her own space. No detail had been left to chance. The walls were covered in posters: Martin Luther King Jr, Che Guevara, the 1965 Freedom Ride, the art from the eighties cover of *The Second Sex*. A rainbow flag was draped over a round mahogany side table. On it was a framed black-and-white photo of Leigh, her husband and two smiling teenagers, along with a vase of dried banksia, ti-tree, palm spears and pampas grasses. Her bookshelf was a treasure trove of works on African American history. An advance copy of her forthcoming book, to be launched in two weeks at an indie bookstore, was prominently displayed.

Leigh wasn't, Ashraf could vouch, one of those insufferable white-saviour feminists. She cared about the academics and students of colour in the faculty, especially women of colour. She'd encouraged Hoang Phan to apply to join the diversity, equity and inclusion committee. She'd started a campus sewing club to counter the fast fashion industry, which, she always emphasised, disproportionately impacted women of the Global South. At the time of the Christchurch terrorist attack, she'd reached out to Ashraf to 'check in', offering support and condolences, which had made him feel seen as a Muslim member of staff – despite the fact he never made a point of parading his background.

It was at an event the Diversity, Equity and Inclusion Committee had organised on campus to send a message of solidarity against Islamophobia and racism that Leigh had introduced Ashraf to Jamal, a master's student at the time, suggesting that Jamal might want to consider pursuing higher degree research and do a PhD with Ashraf.

Now, one year into Jamal's PhD, and Ashraf couldn't have been more satisfied with a student. He had an impeccable work ethic and was undertaking a brilliant, thoroughly under-researched topic ('Interpreting Services in Sydney: A racial analysis').

Yes, Leigh was one of the good ones: solid, walked the walk. She knew he'd been floundering lately, so he couldn't wait to share his news with her.

Ashraf spent the morning poring over articles and policy papers, conducting a rapid review of the literature on countering violent extremism in Australia. It was overwhelming: mountains of research, laws, policies and government grant schemes in the almost twenty years since 9/11. Radicalisation awareness kits, behavioural indicator models and rubrics, case studies, patterns and metrics.

He'd been asked to address the problem of youth radicalisation through a creative project that promoted social inclusion and harmony. The dividends would be making individuals and communities more resilient in refusing extremist ideologies.

But Simon had been adamant that Ashraf shouldn't *explicitly* target any particular segment of the community.

'That would be deeply racist and offensive,' he'd said. 'While we're hoping to cast the net wide and invite young Muslims in particular to engage in a capacity-building, empowering project, we're not here to stigmatise communities.'

The only specific caveat was that Ashraf needed, for ease of finding participants, to *lean towards* focusing on Western Sydney, on suburbs with a higher Muslim population.

'Look at census data,' Simon had suggested. 'And snowball contacts from established groups, organisations and mosques. They're usually best placed to know who needs the extra support.'

'So, find Muslims,' Ashraf had eventually said, 'but don't say I'm looking for Muslims.'

Simon had taken that as a statement, not a question.

14

Hannah adjusted the reeds of her vanilla diffuser, settled into her swivel chair, quickly responded to some messages in the media WhatsApp group about some upcoming snap actions and petitions, and then set out to answer the emails that had pinged into her inbox overnight.

She worked on a story about the rising cost of living and FaceTimed her mother, who was looking after Aya. Aya was napping, so Hannah half listened to her mother complain about how her brother Omar, who lived in Toronto, didn't call enough.

When she asked Hannah to discreetly let him know she was upset but not dare reveal she'd put her up to it, Hannah raised her eyes to the ceiling and took a deep calming breath.

'Of course, Mum,' she reassured her. 'Don't worry, leave it with me.'

A text message notification from Liliana appeared on her phone screen. Hannah gently but firmly ended the call.

Liliana was 'disappointed' with the article: *My quotes have been chopped up or completely cut.*

Hannah hadn't realised her story had just been published. She felt her heart banging inside her chest as she read what had clearly been washed by John in a first edit, and then rinsed by Bev and Patrick, the editorial policies managers.

So this was how it would be. 'Occupied' in scare quotes. 'Israeli mob violence in East Jerusalem' changed to 'clashes'. 'Hamas-run Gaza Ministry of Health' when citing the death toll. 'Apartheid': deleted. Liliana's long quotes giving context and an account of Israel's violence leading to Hamas firing rockets: deleted. '15-year brutal Israeli blockade' changed to 'A blockade imposed by Israel following the election of the terror group Hamas'. 'Israel has killed 35 people including 10 children' changed to '35 people dead'.

On any other piece – any other piece except those relating to Palestine and Israel – all editorial or legal changes, big or small, would be run past her, sometimes to such an annoying degree that she wished they would do it themselves. But, on the rare occasion she wrote about Palestine, they just shoved the edits in or chopped up her writing without consulting her.

She had, in her time at *The Chronicle*, worked out their Hannah-management plan. The preferred approach was to deal with her indirectly. Avoid confrontation.

She'd filed urgent stories and waited for hours for John's response, only for him to come back the next day to say, 'Oh, we need more evidence or more quotes, but it's outdated now so we need to move on.' Or they would kill her story through attrition, like the investigative piece she did on the visa delays reserved only for Palestinian writers invited to NSW Radical Writers' Festival, which John sat on for two weeks, claiming it was with Bev and Patrick, hoping she would either forget or give up. Eventually the story was killed: 'It's too late now. It's not timely.'

They never had the guts to directly reject her pitches or take her off a story. Rather, it was an insidious process of condescension and contempt, dealing with her like she was too angry and fragile for the truth, too emotionally invested to be negotiated with.

Hannah refused to acquiesce to the process. She refused, she refused, she refused.

She bashed out an email to John, pushing back as much as she could for an amendment, substantiating her demand with citations, references to international law, hyperlinks to human rights reports. She wasn't junior enough to be precluded from emailing John, but she also wasn't senior enough for her email to make any difference. No matter. She would do it anyway.

Next: call Liliana and do damage control. Hannah grabbed her phone and hurried across the newsroom, passing John in his corner office huddled with Peter and Nathan around his computer. The office next door was empty. She walked in and closed the door behind her. She sat down, caught her breath and braced herself to speak to Liliana.

She heard Nathan's distinctive laugh through the wall and it both fascinated and irritated her.

She hesitated at the prospect of calling Liliana, feeling nervous and ashamed. She stood again and walked over to the large window overlooking the main road and lost herself in the details below, like the birdshit on the wires, the people walking the streets.

Her stomach suddenly cramped. Some days she could fast until sunset without any sensation of hunger. Some days, like today, her stomach growled and rumbled and she felt every minute. But then she remembered she would be breaking her fast with her mum's cooking tonight and the thought simultaneously excited her (it was always a feast), aroused a pang of guilt (How would people in Gaza, Jamal's family, be breaking their fast amid the bombs and siege?) and made her feel disgusted in herself (enough with the self-flagellation). Oh, she felt so tired! Weary.

Nathan's laugh, and now also Peter's, echoed.

Her eyes, to her shame, prickled.

Allah does not burden a soul beyond that it can bear, she reminded herself. They were words that never failed to soothe her.

She inhaled slowly, then expelled the air hard and fast. She sent a message to Jamal, reminding him to pick up a dessert, and then sat down again and called Liliana.

Liliana's disappointment had turned into resignation: 'I should have expected it.'

Hannah apologised profusely, but then the conversation flipped.

Liliana started counselling Hannah: 'I know that *you* tried your best. I know your intentions. You don't have to apologise.'

Hannah's eyes prickled again and she felt the urge to bawl. She promised she would do better.

'It's not you who needs to do better,' Liliana gently chastised.

On the bus ride home, Hannah was scrolling through LinkedIn when she paused in angry shock.

Peter had reposted a flyer announcement by the Zionist Executive Association of Australia for a 'celebratory wine and cheese + panel' event on 15 May: *The Chronicle*'s Senior Reporter Peter Henderson in conversation with Israel's Ambassador to Australia at High Street Synagogue.

She felt a tremor in her arms. She willed herself to be still and to focus on her breathing, but it didn't last more than a few seconds.

Breathing exercises were for when you dropped a bottle of sauce on a mopped kitchen floor, or when you couldn't find a parking spot at Newtown and the show you booked was about to start. That was when your 4-7-8 came in handy.

What was the breathing exercise to manage the sensation of dread and disgust at knowing that you worked closely with somebody who would be celebrating on the day of your people's Nakba? She was banned from even naming the occupation without the fiction of scare quotes and, as far as her editors were concerned, Gaza was being bombed by the passive voice, but Peter could proudly present at a pro-Israel function?

'There's been a massive wave of statements by academic departments in the US,' Jamal told Hannah over a pot of sage tea at home.

They had not long ago returned from the feast at Hannah's parents' place. Aya was asleep in her cot in her room, and Jamal and Hannah were sitting at the kitchen table. Jamal's laptop was propped open in front of them as they waited for a crisis Zoom meeting with the WhatsApp organising group to start.

Everybody in the group was in a state of frenzy: organising snap actions, rallies, protests, solidarity statements, infographics, social media content, interview opportunities. Jeanette had called the meeting to consolidate their actions, as well as to give each other a chance to vent and grieve outside of WhatsApp messages.

'I've counted over thirty statements so far.'

'Wow, that's incredible,' Hannah said.

'But the academic community here has been silent.' Jamal rested his jaw on the heel of his palm and stared at the counter. 'I think, this is my sense after *six years*, that Australians, maybe especially academics, think they're anti-establishment but are actually, generally, conformists.'

'God, I despise academics,' Hannah said.

'And I despise journalists,' Jamal replied, with a wry smile.

'We need to find a rich tycoon—'

'Who earnt their money ethically,' Jamal interrupted, then took a sip of his tea.

'Yes, of course. And they need to establish a new media organisation and university centre for Palestine studies, no strings attached.'

'You really shouldn't have married for love,' Jamal said drily.

'Ridiculous of me,' Hannah shot back with a laugh.

The laptop pinged, indicating that others had started joining the meeting.

It took all of five minutes for them to begin arguing about the upcoming Nakba rally.

Mikael, who was part of the protest organising group, was concerned about how to control infiltrators hijacking the protest with 'problematic banners and chants'.

'Can we RIP the "Gaza, Gaza, don't you cry" chant?' Jamal said to a chorus of agreement. 'It is, if I am being honest, patronising.'

'We need more marshals,' Mikael emphasised.

Someone else countered: 'I refuse to police people's chants.'

'This respectability politics is all just a useless distraction,' Jeanette said. 'Whatever we say is a problem. Let's focus on the media and the way they're trying to manufacture consent. If I hear this being described as a real estate dispute one more time I will freaking lose my mind.'

'Have you noticed how Nabil's case is overshadowing coverage of Israel's bombing?' Mikael said.

'We have to do something,' Hannah added.

They created a Google doc and drafted an open letter for journalists, media workers, writers and commentators to sign. Jeanette, by far the most digitally proficient, set up a website called *Do Better.* By midnight, they had emailed the open letter to as many people in the media industry as they knew.

Hannah's name was the first on the list.

15

Barnaby sent an all-staff email to the Faculty of Social Sciences warmly congratulating Ashraf on his Youth Power project just before lunchtime. Congratulatory emails started to flow in. Ashraf saved them into a folder he titled 'Collegial Feedback'.

There was a knock on the door. He looked up and saw Jamal. He waved him in.

Jamal stepped inside.

Ashraf was startled by how drawn he appeared, by the dark shadows under his red-rimmed eyes, by his unkempt hair. He was usually impeccably presented.

'Are you okay?' Ashraf asked with concern. But as he asked, he realised how stupid he'd been, how insensitive. He had forgotten Jamal was from Gaza, that his family was there. 'I mean,' he said, embarrassed, 'I know you're not okay. Forgive the automatic question. Have you heard from your family?'

Jamal threw his backpack, covered in Free Palestine badges, on the floor and plonked himself into the chair. His right leg jiggled up and down relentlessly.

'We lost contact last night.'

'My God.'

'But they texted me this morning. They're alive. For now.'

'I'm so sorry, Jamal,' said Ashraf. 'Do you want to take time off? Put in some personal leave?'

'No,' Jamal said. 'I need to keep myself busy. Now is the time to mobilise.'

He took his phone out of his pocket, fiddled with it and then passed it to Ashraf.

'Have a read,' he said. 'I'm going to email it to all the faculty. Law and Education too. If you have contacts in Engineering, can you forward it to them?'

Ashraf saw the title and winced. He skimmed and scrolled to the end. There was no need to read the details. This document had to be killed.

Jamal was his PhD student. He would be tainted by association. But not for a minute was this about self-interest alone. He was, no word of a lie, genuinely concerned for Jamal too. Jamal had worked so hard to be here. What is it they said at the protests? From Gaza to Gadigal? That was Jamal, *literally*. And now he wanted to ask people to sign this BDS call? The only signature JBU was interested in was the one that Ancient History signed last year on a three-year MOU with Hebrew University. Or the signature on the contract between the university and Elbit.

Jamal was not going to save Gaza this way. He was asking for giant leaps on Palestine when, quite frankly, people needed to be allowed to take baby steps. BDS was a grenade. Nobody with a mortgage or a landlord was going to throw that into their workplace. And anyway, the arc of the moral universe was long et cetera.

Ashraf turned his chair to face Jamal and crossed his legs. He would be mentor, peer and Arab uncle. If all else failed, he'd pull rank and go PhD supervisor on him.

'This is excellent,' he said, switching to Arabic. Jamal must comprehend that he was on his side.

Jamal stared at Ashraf solemnly.

'It sets out the case flawlessly. Nobody can dispute it on factual grounds. But unfortunately, Jamal, this is too risky. The university has indicated in the past that it views calls for academic boycotts as antisemitic.'

'We have to push back,' Jamal said, his eyes flashing.

'Yes, but slowly. Things don't change with one statement. We're the people of steadfastness, no?'

'Sumud until we're exterminated?'

Ashraf allowed Jamal to sit with his anger for a moment, then said: 'Revolution isn't a one-time event – Audre Lorde.'

'Ashraf! Gaza doesn't need BrainyQuote.com. It needs our action.'

Ashraf lowered his eyes in embarrassment. Then, after another pause, he adjusted his approach. 'Wallahi, Jamal, I understand your pain. Remember Lebanon in 2006? Or maybe you don't. You would have been … how old?'

'Twelve. But twelve in Gaza. Different.'

Ashraf cleared his throat. 'I was at Sydney Uni then. Thirty-four days I walked those university grounds like a zombie. I had to patiently explain and justify and hold back. You're just starting your academic life. You're still a student. You have no power—'

'That's just the point though, isn't it?' Jamal said calmly but forcefully. 'This place, all of it, is built to make everyone think they have no power. We're all supposed to accept being atomised and fragmented. But you *do* have power. Leigh has power. And even I have power. Maybe it's not much. But I believe in it, and I refuse to surrender it. I'm *alive* and *here* and that means something.'

'Let's think, then, of how you can act in a way that does not risk everything. Yes, you are *here*. Against all odds, ya Jamal! From Khan Younis to JBU. We need to keep you here, from PhD to post-doc and on and on. That's why Leigh introduced us. She saw in you what I see. Like it or not, these institutions are not ready for BDS and you didn't go through all this struggle to throw it away with a petition. Focus on what you can do safely instead of jeopardising the little power you have.'

Jamal stood up abruptly and walked to the window. 'What would you have me do? They're trapped and expected to shut up and accept. They rattle their cage a little and F-15s drop US bombs down on them.'

'Your job here is to bring people to your side, Jamal. You and I both know there's a cost to supporting this cause. You need to be strategic. Give people a way to show their support without compromising their already precarious jobs.'

'Solidarity in the shadows isn't solidarity. It's cowardice.'

'Yes, I understand that you see it that way. But with restructures constantly on the horizon, maybe we also need to be a little more understanding about the context in which you are asking for solidarity.'

'The context is genocide.'

'That's not language that will advance your cause.'

'The context is seventy-three years of ethnic cleansing, colonisation and apartheid.'

'Invest time in mobilising more people.'

'I don't *have* time. My family is in Gaza *right now* trying to survive bombs.'

Ashraf didn't want to appear unsympathetic, but he was losing patience. This dogmatic, purist, single-minded attitude was the death of every Arab and Muslim movement because they were fucking useless at building critical mass and didn't understand that Palestine would be a bad investment until enough people made it a good one.

There was no way that would happen if they refused to play by the rules of the game, to find a way to work the system.

'You're on a scholarship, Jamal,' Ashraf said. 'And I'm advising you as your supervisor: find another way and I will support you.'

Jamal opened his mouth to push back, but Ashraf raised his hand to stop him. It had occurred to him that there was a way to make good on this.

'In fact, Jamal, I've just been given an incredible opportunity. You want to do meaningful work? It's in the grassroots. In community. Help the refugees who are here in front of you. The group you work with? Out at Canterbury? Let's chat about how we can connect them with my project and be real change-makers, hey?'

16

Hannah had been unable to find any mutual contacts with Nabil or his family. She reached out to a prominent imam at the closest mosque to Nabil's home, but he'd never met Nabil or his parents.

'He's probably receiving advice and care from a community leader,' the imam told her, his voice strained. 'But nobody is going to talk to you or anybody in the media. They need to focus on his legal case.'

Hannah knew that he was right. The national media, politicians across the spectrum, public commentators and lobby groups had all judged Nabil as guilty. Perhaps it was a good thing that Nabil and his family remained silent. As for Al-Bayinnah, that was, maybe, a story where some semblance of truth-telling could be achieved.

Peter made a beeline for Hannah as soon as she arrived at the office. He informed her that he was writing a piece reporting a 'high level of staff disunity and disharmony at Al-Bayyinah' – even though, she noted, the only teacher he had on the record was the single (anonymous) ex-employee.

'Can you at least let me follow a few leads?' Hannah asked and placed her bag in her desk drawer. 'Find more teachers?'

'Sure,' Peter said with a look of gratitude. 'The more the better.'

Hannah tilted her head to the side. She tried to maintain a polite, deferential tone commensurate with his seniority. 'If the problem is systemic,' she said, 'I guess it's not just better to have more than one but necessary …' She trailed off.

Peter ignored her. It was wild how infantilising he could be without him even realising it.

If she was being honest with herself, she had to admit that Peter wasn't ignoring her out of malevolence. He was so earnest, so self-idealising, so genuinely convinced of the superiority of his worldview that, as far as Hannah could discern, he just didn't register her dissent or critique in intellectual terms. It was, to him, all identity politics.

He couldn't imagine that things should be any different or that there was a problem with the way things were. He believed in the establishment, in the liberal bullshit project of objectivity, balance and neutrality, and if Hannah pushed back he seemed to always convey the impression that he believed it was because her identity prevented her from truly understanding the system.

'I've also got quotes from some police officers who say, anonymously, that they had concerns about radicalisation at the school,' Peter said.

'What were their concerns?'

'They can't elaborate. But it's still a strong, authoritative quote.'

'But is that fair?' Hannah raised her voice a little but then quickly brought it down. 'I mean, if you put that in an article and it's given this weight of authority, how do readers know the concerns aren't based on racist assumptions? Should we be giving the police the benefit of the doubt here?'

A frown creased Peter's forehead. 'Oh, no, of course we don't give anybody the benefit of the doubt. I'm getting an expert to define radicalisation so that there's some context to balance that statement.' Then he smiled and said: 'I'm experienced enough to be able to judge whether a source is credible or not.'

Hannah let out a humourless laugh. 'So we're at the police-are-a-credible-source-on-the-reputation-of-Islamic-schools stage.' *Damn. Too sassy?* She had to control herself.

Peter was either too gormless or considered himself too superior to her to even discern her sarcasm. 'The principal refused to run a deradicalisation program,' he continued.

'A principal of an Islamic school rejects the criminalisation of her students,' Hannah said, deadpan.

'You know, Hannah, I admire your passion,' Peter pivoted.

Hannah dug her nails into her hand.

'I mean it,' he insisted. 'You care about your community.'

'I care about the truth,' Hannah said quietly.

'So do I. And I don't begrudge you asking questions and being critical. For bringing your unique perspective and healthy scepticism to this.'

She wanted to vomit.

'I appreciate that our vantage point differs but also that this story may feel more personal for you.'

Before Hannah had a chance to respond, John emerged from his office and signalled to Hannah. She was glad for the escape route. She walked over and hovered for a moment near the doorway.

John pointed at the seat in front of his wide, glass desk. He took a handful out of a small packet of trail mix, his gaze fixed on his computer screen. He would be with her in a minute, he told her. Hannah took note of a 2012 Walkley award perched on a beechwood sideboard, beside a photograph of John with his Korean partner, Daniel, and their daughter, who they'd adopted as an infant around the same time Hannah started working at *The Chronicle*. Hannah waited for a few moments until he eventually spoke.

'Hannah,' John said, interlacing his fingers and resting them on his lap. 'You're aware of our social media policy?'

Hannah nodded.

He sighed. 'It was brought to my attention that you've been posting about the conflict in Gaza on your LinkedIn account.'

'Brought to your attention, as in a complaint?'

'Yes.'

'By who?'

'Sorry, that's confidential.' John turned his screen around to show Hannah. 'There are two posts of concern, Hannah. Yesterday you shared a post by Mahmoud Kurd.'

'Mohammed El-Kurd,' Hannah corrected him.

'Okay, er, yes. Anyway, you shared his post. He says, "I am sick of living under their fascist rule" – and by "their" we can presume he is referring to Israel.'

'Yes.'

'That exposes you as being somebody who isn't impartial. You are effectively, by sharing his post, accepting his construction of Israel as a fascist state.'

'Do you know who he is?'

John looked at her blankly. 'Is that relevant?'

Hannah tried to control her voice. 'Yes. Mohammed is *from* Sheikh Jarrah. Did you read the rest of his tweet?'

'It's irrelevant to the question of impartiality.'

'But, sorry, um … ' Hannah paused. She had to push back, but she was excruciatingly conscious of her every word. 'With all due respect, I think … I think that's the wrong question. Mohammed is a direct witness. His home was stolen by settlers. He's describing the violence and punishing blockade inflicted on his neighbourhood.'

'Your responsibility is to remain objective and impartial. In your second post you reposted a tweet by somebody sharing a Human Rights Watch report that accuses Israel of committing the crime of apartheid.'

Hannah blinked, baffled by what she was hearing. 'Yes. A Human Rights Watch report. Hardly the Hamas charter.'

'Reliance on Human Rights Watch reports aren't sufficient as there are debates about the interpretation of laws and the impartiality of such organisations. As a reporter with us, you need to be perceived as balanced and factual. The tweet you reposted also used the hashtag *#Gazaunderattack*.'

Hannah felt like she would split asunder. 'But Gaza *is* under attack,' she said quietly.

'We need to remain balanced, Hannah.'

'One of the first things I learnt at uni was that if someone says it's raining and another person says it's dry, it's not my job to quote them both. It's my job to look out of the window and see which is true.'

John gave her a condescending smile. 'The Israel–Palestinian conflict is hardly a weather forecast.'

She started to respond but he raised his hand.

'And sharing a hashtag like that welds you to an explicit ideological position. It's the very definition of taking sides.'

'When the report was released,' Hannah said, 'you ran a piece by the CEO of the Zionist Executive Association of Australia, trashing the report.'

John's posture stiffened. 'An *opinion* piece.'

'And rejected an op-ed pitched by a Palestinian lawyer responding to the same report. Is that the kind of "both sides" you mean?'

John looked on the verge of losing his temper. But he was too good a liberal to let the mask drop. 'Look, Hannah, we're here to protect your position at *The Chronicle* and ensure you can keep on doing the excellent work you do. I appreciate this is difficult for you, but you've exposed yourself to credible accusations of pro-Palestinian bias—'

'I'm not pro-Palestinian,' Hannah interrupted, trying to control her voice. 'I *am* Palestinian.'

John seemed startled by Hannah's tone. He cleared his throat nervously. 'You're in breach of the social media policy, Hannah,' he said slowly, speaking to her like a nurse might speak to a hysterical patient. 'I'll need you to delete both posts.'

She stood up. 'Fine,' she said through gritted teeth.

Hannah forced herself to walk calmly out of John's office, all the way to her cubicle. She sank into her chair and opened her laptop.

Hell is empty, she thought, *and all the devils are here.*

That evening after dinner, Jamal rinsed dishes at the kitchen sink and handed them to Hannah to put in the dishwasher.

'I asked you to take the washing out of the machine before you left this morning,' Hannah scolded.

'Yes, I forgot, sorry,' Jamal said.

Aya was fussing and squirming in her highchair.

‘Now we have to re-wash them and they won’t dry in time for tomorrow,’ Hannah said.

Jamal rinsed a fistful of cutlery and passed it to Hannah.

Aya squealed, making her displeasure at being left in her highchair known.

‘Aya, stop whingeing!’ Hannah cried. ‘I can’t be expected to think about every little thing.’

She threw a fork into the cutlery holder, stormed over to Aya and picked her up roughly.

‘I forgot!’ Jamal called after her.

Hannah took Aya to the bathroom. She ran the bath, undressed her at the change table and slowly lowered her into the water. Hannah knelt down and gently rinsed her chubby body.

‘I’m sorry, baby girl,’ she whispered to Aya, who was already splashing and kicking with delight.

Later, with Aya fast asleep in her cot, Hannah plonked herself down on the couch beside Jamal, ripped into a packet of Tim Tams and started browsing through Netflix.

‘I’ve been asked to speak at the Nakba rally,’ Jamal said, looking up from his phone.

‘Great,’ Hannah said. ‘I’ll ask Mum to take Aya so we can go together.’ She groaned dramatically. ‘There’s nothing to watch.’

‘Guess what?’ Jamal said.

Hannah, eyes on the screen, grunted in response.

'One hundred signatures and that's solely through the group's internal circulation.'

Hannah threw the remote aside and straightened up. 'No way!'

She whipped out her phone and scrutinised the list of signatories, yelling out names and comments every few seconds: 'No way *he* signed!' 'Oh my God, she's the *last* person I expected!' 'Who is this person? I love that I don't know everyone.' Hannah gave Jamal an excited peck on the mouth and said: 'We'll go public with it soon.' Then she half laughed. 'RIP my job.'

'I'd like to see the guys who've been on pro-Israel lobby-sponsored junkets try to play the *you need to be neutral* line.'

'This list is only going to grow,' Hannah said. 'They can't ignore us.'

17

Jamal must have been waiting for Ashraf at the café because he hurried towards him as soon as he joined the queue.

'Okay, you win. No BDS,' Jamal declared. 'I've drafted a solidarity statement.' He handed Ashraf his phone, which was open on a Google document.

Ashraf pretended to read it intently while he instead searched for excuses because there was no way he could sign this. Every word was a trigger: genocide, apartheid, settler colonialism, rogue state, right of return, US-led imperialism. But at least no call for an academic boycott.

'This is excellent, Jamal,' he said, covering up his lie with a generous smile, broad enough to convey he was impressed but still proportionate to the gravity of the situation.

Jamal seemed pleased.

For a moment, Ashraf pitied him, having to sublimate anger and grief into the politics of respectability and palpability, to condense a cause into an eloquent rant.

But here, at least, was something tangible. Jamal could gather his signatures, publish the statement on social media and perhaps in an online publication for the already converted to read, and then, yes, he could proudly say he had achieved something.

He offered Jamal the names of some academics at other universities ('cross-institutional solidarity is important') but explained, with sincere regret and a sigh for extra effect, that given his recent consultancy project with the government, he was not at liberty to sign any political statements.

'That makes it even more important for us to ensure this project *for* and *with* our community is a success,' Ashraf said.

Jamal provided Ashraf with an update on some potential participants. He had been offering voluntary interpreting services at a community centre with newly arrived refugees. Some of the parents had children in their late teens, early twenties. They were keen to do something creative or sporty. And it was free. Always a bonus.

Ashraf was zoning in and out of a curriculum capstone restructure meeting with Leigh and a few others across the faculty.

Dave was an external consultant with no curriculum or teaching experience who was being paid the price of a Tesla to tell the academics and curriculum experts how they should design their units. Droning on about the importance of making the e-learning site more 'visually appealing', he took out a pink sticky note and a black sharpie, wrote *visual appeal DYNAMIC!* on the note and stuck it on a large piece of butcher's paper he had taped to the whiteboard.

'You need to engage students,' he continued. 'But tailor the experience to them too. For example, you could introduce a quiz at the beginning of the term where the students are asked about their aims in the unit – do they want to pass or get a high distinction? And depending on their answer the site opens at a particular level. The students who answer "pass" get a lighter and easier load tailored to that level of ambition and the students who say they want a high distinction get a tougher load.'

Leigh locked a conspiratorial eye with Ashraf and he fought back an urge to laugh.

Dave finally opened the session up for questions.

'Are these suggestions or compulsory changes?'

'Isn't the goal to raise the bar and encourage our students to aim high?'

'The e-learning site is always crashing. Could we maybe spend resources into making it reliable instead of pretty?'

While Dave visibly steeled himself, Ashraf zoned out again. He opened his laptop to check his emails.

Last night he'd sent Simon a proposal for a zine-making project. Participants would use digital technologies to create their own zines, published as online flipbooks, using them as 'an artistic vessel in which to experiment with political and cultural expression thereby fostering healthy civic participation'.

Simon had written back.

Ashraf felt his heart thumping – and then felt rather foolish that his heart was thumping – as he opened the email. He started reading and couldn't help but break into a goofy grin. Simon was 'impressed' and 'supportive of this project proposal'.

Ashraf started drafting a reply but was interrupted by Leigh, who leant in close and said in a low, concerned voice: 'Did you see Jamal's email?'

He shook his head. He went back to his inbox. Jamal had sent an email an hour ago, addressed to each university faculty email, cc-ing him, subject line: *Gaza solidarity statement*. Ashraf pressed his lips together as he read it.

Dear colleagues and peers,

We are in the fifth day of Israel's relentless bombing of Gaza following a month (and continuing) of brutal violence against Palestinians in occupied East Jerusalem, the West Bank and across Israel. **Please find here** a statement of solidarity with Palestine from academics in Australian universities. Please add your signature to join many esteemed colleagues in taking a stand.

Kind regards,
Jamal Abdul-Hamid

PhD Candidate (Supervisor: Dr Ashraf Magdy)
Tutor, Middle East Politics
Department of Politics
JBU
I acknowledge that I work and study on the traditional and unceded lands of the Gadigal people.

Ashraf felt a wave of nausea. He sampled the stream of replies.

Some were supportive: 'Please add my name'; 'Thank you for inviting me to be part of this important solidarity initiative'. Several asked the sender to be removed: 'Take me off this list immediately'; 'Please consider whether this statement is in breach of the university's Freedom of Speech and Academic Freedom Policy and remove me from this email chain now'. Others were outraged: 'This statement is a disgrace. Where in this statement do you mention Hamas's rockets? A shockingly inhumane omission'; 'The loss of civilian life is tragic, whether Israeli or Palestinian. Except Israel does everything it can to avoid civilian deaths, unlike Hamas which deliberately uses its people as human shields'; 'This is an inappropriate and unprofessional use of university email'.

Jamal had fucked up. Monumentally fucked up.

Leigh motioned to the door, indicating they should talk privately. They excused themselves and left.

'I understand Jamal must be very distressed,' Leigh said, arms folded across her lemon linen dress. 'It's a very challenging time. But this was reckless.'

'Yes, I know,' Ashraf said. 'And he *cc-ed* me!'

'Yes, regrettably.'

'I cautioned him.'

'It just doesn't help the situation,' Leigh said, with the slightly wounded and weary air of someone who had endured many meetings drafting glossy policies nobody followed. 'A statement like this leaves no room for nuance,' she continued. 'I understand that nuance is the least of Jamal's concerns. He's naturally entitled to take a partisan approach. But this is a highly complex conflict and sharing that statement to all staff has caused offence to those who, understandably, have their own version of the conflict.'

Guilty regret swept over Ashraf. He should have been clearer in his counsel. He should have discerned how vulnerable Jamal was at this time and that he would be more susceptible to rash decisions. Decisions that had effects beyond Jamal, because Ashraf was explicitly – gallingly – tethered to Jamal in being both cc-ed to the email and featured in the email signature.

Ashraf ran his hands through his hair and leant back against the wall, staring up at the ceiling. He didn't need this controversy now. He didn't need a knock on the door from Barnaby, the dean, only days after he'd finally managed to resuscitate his career.

'I can speak to Jamal,' Leigh offered gently. 'And I'll handle Barnaby, let him know you had nothing to do with this. As research director, it might be better coming from me.'

'Maybe you're right.'

'We can discuss ways Jamal can feel supported while being mindful of the importance of taking an even-handed, careful, evidence-based approach.'

'Agreed.'

That evening, as Ashraf sat down to eat a takeaway curry, an email pinged into his phone inbox.

Dear staff,

In future, access to all-staff faculty email lists will be restricted to executive management and departmental administrators.

I would like to remind all staff, postgrad students and professional staff that University mailing lists must be used within the context of the University's policies and practices. Please remember to follow the university's Email and Internet Procedures. I draw your attention to clause 15.2.

Kind regards,
Alex Berman
Arts Executive Dean

18

Hannah's phone alerted her to an email. It was an advisory from the NSW Joint Counter Terrorism Team announcing a press conference at 8 am. Nabil had been charged.

Within moments, John called. 'Get out there and then to Fairfield court,' he said. 'Peter will be there too. There's no way they've granted bail. Try your hardest to get something from family, friends. Find someone who will talk.'

Hannah caught an Uber to the NSW Police Executive Office in Elizabeth Street. The press gallery was full and she was about to sit in one of the few remaining available seats towards the back when she noticed Peter in the front row. She walked down the aisle towards him, but he hadn't saved her a spot. He saw her and gave a nod of recognition, no hint of an apology at leaving her standing alone. She turned and stalked towards the back row to sit beside a court reporter she recognised from *The Daily Telegraph*.

Commissioner Caitlin Drebb took to the stage and stood behind the podium. Her dirty-blonde hair was held in a tight low bun under her police hat.

'Last night, NSW's Joint Counter Terrorism Team, which includes the Australian Federal Police, NSW Police, Australian Secruity Intelligence Organisation and the NSW Crime Commission, interviewed eighteen-year-old Nabil Mostafa,' she began.

She was a small, slight woman and she spoke slowly and cautiously, with the air of somebody who – ironically, given her position – didn't like public speaking.

'The man was subsequently charged with a Commonwealth terrorism offence as a result of his alleged involvement in the occupation and protest that took place at Joseph Banks University on 5 May.'

Hannah looked around the room. The air was heavy with anticipation, scandal, excitement.

She'd seen Nabil's JBU livestream circulating all over again on social media that morning. Nabil wasn't a *man*. He was a boy, a high school student. She felt the weight of that word on Nabil as viscerally as if it were a boulder sinking his body deeper and deeper into water.

'His bail has been refused,' the commissioner said, 'and he will be attending local court today to determine bail. We will allege that during the illegal occupation and protest the alleged offender filmed himself holding the flag of a proscribed terrorist organisation and wore an item of clothing widely recognised as a symbol of that organisation, with a message embroidered on it expressly professing support for armed struggle.'

It's a fucking UN resolution, Hannah thought.

'He has been charged with advocating terrorism under section 80.2C of the *Criminal Code Act 1995*, which carries a maximum penalty of five years.'

Five years? My God.

Hannah took a deep breath. What were the consequences for the people who sent her emails or messages on Twitter, threatening her with death and rape after stories she'd written about Muslims or Arabs?

She was told to 'ignore the trolls', never mind that one of them had attended the office and demanded to meet with her. He was escorted out of the building by security and Hannah was advised to take a few days off and 'lie low'.

At last year's Nakba rally, a man holding an Israeli flag had deliberately pushed into her and her friends, called her a *sharmouta* and made a throat-slitting motion – all in view of the police, who did nothing.

She could feel her heart pounding as the press conference continued.

'On 5 May, investigators from the joint counterterrorism team completed search warrants at the alleged offender's home where a number of items were seized, including the alleged offender's electronic devices,' the commissioner said. 'I'd like to reassure the community and especially students and staff in the university sector, that the police are here to keep them safe. Based on our investigations, we are confident that this was a lone case, and that the accused isn't connected to any terror cell, either here or overseas.'

Terror cell? Hannah wanted to scream. *He was more likely part of a study cell.*

The commissioner opened for questions.

Peter's hand shot up and, perfectly positioned in the front row, the commissioner nodded at him.

'How confident are you that he was not groomed or radicalised by people close to him in his community or school?'

'This matter will go through the justice system while we continue our investigations, but we are confident that the accused acted alone.'

Hannah raised her hand, but she didn't stand much of a chance all the way at the back.

'Will you be seeking the maximum penalty?' another reporter asked, to which the commissioner replied that she couldn't comment on sentencing.

There were questions about the other protesters ('They have been separately and differently charged given the circumstances of their participation.') and whether this case would 'push the government to reform the law to proscribe *all* of Hamas', which the commissioner said was 'a question for the government and parliament' and that 'our job is to enforce the law as it currently stands'.

Hannah kept waving her hand and had almost given up when the commissioner finally pointed to her.

'Let's get one in from the back of the room,' she said.

'Thank you, Commissioner,' Hannah began. 'As

I understand it, the headband was green, but it had the numbers of a UN resolution on self-determination and the right to armed struggle. It wasn't an actual Hamas headband. So that leaves the flag. Does this mean that the act of holding the Hamas flag – and my understanding is that it isn't an illegal symbol – amounts to advocating terrorism?'

'In these circumstances, the facts together, the alleged offender's actions, we argue, amounted to advocating terrorism.' The commissioner drew a breath. 'I want to reiterate to the public that our work isn't finished. Our excellent community liaison teams are meeting with community leaders and schools of faith over the coming days to provide support, answer questions and provide assurances that we target criminality, not communities, and we investigate radicalisation, not religion.'

Later that day, Hannah stood on the steps of Fairfield Local Court waiting with a throng of other reporters and TV camera crews for Nabil to emerge from the closed bail hearing, feeling she was covering a story she was a part of. A visit to the Registrar's Office for court documents had disclosed that bail had been denied and Nabil would be remanded in custody.

When Nabil eventually stepped out, flanked by two police officers, the reporters and camera crew, overwhelmingly Anglo, charged forward, shouting out:

'Do you support Hamas?', 'Are you fighting the charges?', 'Do you have any regrets?' and 'How will this affect your studies?'

Nabil, in a charcoal suit and bright-white Nike Airs, looked pale, frightened. His face was clean-shaven, his cheeks and chin revealing small clusters of teenage acne. He kept his eyes fixed on the ground as the police escorted him through the frenzied horde of reporters.

Hannah knew she should be vying for a place in the crowd, pushing herself forward to ask a question, but she stood frozen to her spot, revolted by the entire scene.

As she watched the police carefully guide Nabil into the police car, she saw him raise his handcuffed hands slightly and gesture a half-wave to a small group standing behind one of the white pillars of the courthouse, a few steps from her.

The middle-aged woman in a white hijab and burgundy pants suit was, the resemblance obvious, his mother. She waved back, a look of agony on her face, and the man standing beside her, Nabil's father Hannah presumed, put his arm around his wife as he gave Nabil a firm nod, as if trying to encourage him to stay strong. Two young men, Hannah guessed they were in their late twenties and might have been Nabil's brothers or cousins, stood with them, looking nervous, clearly trying to be stoic. Nabil's lawyer turned to face the huddle of the family when the doors of the police car had all been closed and it finally pulled away from the kerb.

It seemed Hannah wasn't the only one to notice the family connection. As soon as Nabil was gone, a reporter, followed by a pushy cameraman from Channel 9, launched at Nabil's mother: 'How do you feel about your son being refused bail?'

Nabil's lawyer immediately led Nabil's parents away from the scene, ignoring the reporters chasing them, yelling out questions.

Hannah shifted her handbag to her other shoulder. She took a few steps when she overheard the two men who had been standing with Nabil's parents speaking in Arabic. They were lamenting the court's decision, discussing who would do an interview with *A Current Story*, one of the most sensationalised, tabloid current-affairs programs on TV.

Hannah wasn't an impulsive person and yet she felt compelled to interrupt the men. She introduced herself in Arabic and, before they had a chance to register a response, said, perhaps a little too forcefully, 'Don't speak to the media. Especially *A Current Story*.'

One man's forehead wrinkled in confusion and opened his mouth to say something but stopped. The other man looked her up and down with his big hazel eyes, intrigued. In a suspicious voice, he asked, 'Who are you?'

'A journalist,' Hannah replied, provoking even more bewilderment. She stepped forward and lowered her voice. 'Which is why I'm telling you there's no mainstream media outlet,' and here she paused, gesturing to the media crowd that was beginning to disperse now that Nabil and his parents had left, 'that's going to tell Nabil's story the way you hope for it to be told.'

Hannah knew that she was throwing away a chance at a story, the kind of story that launches careers. She knew that if John or Peter got wind of what she was doing she'd be in real trouble, maybe lose her job. She didn't care.

The hazel-eyed man folded his arms across his chest and gave Hannah a sceptical look.

Hannah picked up the scent of oud aftershave, either an expensive brand or an imitation label like the ones they sold at the kiosk in front of Aldi Merrylands.

'You Muslim?' the other man asked gruffly.

Hannah nodded. 'And Palestinian.'

The effect of her reply was instantaneous. The men's faces suddenly brightened and their bodies relaxed.

Hannah led them around the corner to a more private space to talk.

They introduced themselves as Nabil's first cousins: Samih, the oud-smelling man, and Bilal.

Nabil had 'changed' after visiting their family in Ein El Hilweh refugee camp in Lebanon last year, Bilal explained, as he took out a vape and started puffing. 'It was like he couldn't settle down back into his life,' Bilal said.

Hannah nodded, discreetly waving away the cloud of what smelt like rockmelon, but didn't interrupt.

'He's just a teenager,' Samih added flatly. 'But he felt

guilty that we're here and they're there, you know?'

'But also angry,' Bilal said, between urgent puffs. 'Like, we're all obviously angry. But we donate and go on with our lives, you know? What can we do? Really?'

'Nabil wasn't like that,' Samih said. He looked into her eyes with desperate determination. 'He couldn't switch off. He got involved in that group. He said it was better than doing nothing.'

'It's a fucking joke,' Bilal threw out angrily. 'He's an idiot for holding the flag, but he wasn't promoting terrorism or whatever they're saying about him. He was protesting that weapons group.'

'You really don't think the media wants to hear our point of view?' Samih asked, rubbing his long neck.

Hannah turned to them one at a time. 'No.' Feeling bad for them, she took out her card. 'Here's my number. If you need any help or advice, don't hesitate to call me.'

Bilal took and examined the card, then dialled the number.

Hannah's phone buzzed.

'Now you have mine', he said. 'Save it, just in case.'

Hannah went from the courthouse to a meeting with a parent from Al-Bayinnah that she'd arranged while at work yesterday. The parent, Natalia, had agreed to speak to her on condition of anonymity. They agreed to meet at Sweetie

Cakes, a café not far from the school, an hour before Natalia had to pick up her kids from their after-school Robotics class.

Hannah chose a booth in the corner, away from the group of mums and noisy toddlers near the window and the bored-looking support worker sitting beside an elderly man in a wheelchair, scrolling on her phone as she chewed gum loudly.

Natalia was tall and chubby, dressed in an emerald-green salwar kameez and loose chiffon hijab, some hair falling down her forehead. She had a luminous face and was animated, bristling with energy, every muscle of her face activated as she spoke at a pace and with an intensity that left little chance for Hannah to interject.

'My daughter's in Year 11. We've been at Al-Bayinnah since she was in Year 3.'

Hannah moved her phone closer to Natalia to make sure, in the crowded café, that the recording picked up her voice.

'I've known Ms Sayid since Sohaila started. Ms Sayid's strict, yes, but fair. And she refuses, okay, to run the school on a selective system, like many other Islamic schools – kicking kids out if they don't get top marks.'

As Natalia took a breath and a sip of her iced coffee, Hannah jumped in. 'There are allegations that there were concerns about so-called radicalised students at the school – a culture of downplaying the problem, beyond Nabil. Were you aware of any chatter, as a parent?'

Natalia's eyes flashed. She sat up taller in her chair and

adjusted her hijab. 'No! This is all just the media. They lie and twist the truth.'

'Oh, I agree,' Hannah rushed to reassure her. 'I'm just asking questions so I know how to counter the angle, um, others are pursuing. Nabil was arrested for occupying a university building with a direct-action group. Do you think that—'

'The media and politicians are painting him as a crazy fanatic. But maybe he did that because nobody would listen to him.'

'Was he given a safe space to talk at Al-Bayinnah? I mean, is it a safe space to talk?'

'Look, Ms Sayid has always been very encouraging. It's a safe space. My other daughter's at Trinity – my ex pays her school fees, so why not? – and she received the principal's award for an essay on the … what was it called … the Aboriginal Ceremony Passport, I think. Do you know it?' Hannah didn't have a chance to respond. 'They did it for the refugees.'

Natalia took a beat, and Hannah nodded for her to continue.

'So her essay was all about being Pakistani, that's where we're from, and the passport ceremony and the Aboriginal peoples being the first peoples of this land. Anyway, it was a beautiful essay and she got the principal's award, but then guess what? On Harmony Day, Umber wears salwar kameez and a keffiyeh on top, it's Free Palestine always in our house, and the principal makes her take the keffiyeh off and put it in her bag. Can you believe it?' Natalia banged her hands on the table. Her glass shifted slightly and she grabbed it. 'Al-Bayinnah is different and I'm glad of it.'

Trying not to be subsumed by the quick running currents of Natalia's account, Hannah asked, 'What about other parents? How do they feel?'

'I don't know.' Natalia laughed. 'We're a big school. Some will like politics, others won't. We send our kids to an Islamic school because we want that space for our kids to practise their deen, not get bullied, okay? Also, especially nowadays with all the alphabet haram in schools. LQBXYZ and so on.'

Hannah frowned. 'But queer kids get bullied. Surely we should be compassionate and sympathise—'

'Nobody should be bullied. My heart breaks for them. But I don't want my kids confused.'

Hannah was about to respond, but Natalia ploughed on.

'Anyway, many of us are very upset about what's happened to Nabil. He's in Year 12, too. What will this mean for his future? But many of us parents are terrified. It's better for kids to avoid politics, keep their heads down to study.' Natalia glanced at her watch and leapt to her feet. 'I need to get going to get a good car spot.'

Hannah walked Natalia out of the café, reassuring her that any quotes she used would be anonymously attributed.

19

His phone was buzzing on the eve of Eid. A barrage of chain messages filled with Happy Eid graphics, greeting cards in Arabic and English, funny memes (Eid-Mubarak with a picture of Barack Obama), gifs of crescent moons and mosques with catchy tunes. The barrage included, he was pleasantly surprised, a message from Fayza. A family photo with a 'Happy Eid from the Sayid family' caption, personalised with an additional message: 'We're doing Eid prayers at Heartlands Mosque, join us if you're free (7 am). Salams.'

Ashraf had just finished the tedious university ethics application and consent forms he was required to submit and have approved before he could start his project. But he was so excited that he had thrown himself into the task. Meanwhile, Jamal had secured a group of participants and would help run the project.

After submitting the application and forwarding a copy to Simon as a courtesy, Ashraf closed his laptop and went out to his balcony for some fresh air. He pulled out his phone, now free to scroll without guilt, and was immediately consumed by the footage of Israel's relentless bombing campaign in al-Rimal neighbourhood. The death toll was now over one hundred.

The horror of it all turned his mind to his daughters. He sent them a voice note on WhatsApp. Then he started swiping through their photos.

He ached for them. There were times he would be at his desk at work, or stuck in traffic, and he would be struck by the sudden terror that they had been in an accident. He would sit in that feeling, in the briefest thought that his daughters were dead, and be overcome by panic and nausea.

They were no longer in his immediate world. They were a wi-fi signal, faces on a screen. If he had known there would be an expiry date on being an active, present father, he would have quit his job and spent every day with them as children.

He was beyond the days of missing Mya now. Missing was no longer an apt word. It suggested something done *to* somebody such that they are unjustly extricated from one's life. Mya was not missing. She had removed herself. She had exercised her choice and severed all ties beyond the most life-sustaining: those to their daughters.

Any nostalgia for the life that they had built together – and that was the point, that he wanted to keep doing that, here and now, whereas she was fixated on building a life in the hereafter – had been replaced with confusion, hurt and resentment so bitter he could taste it like her always-burnt bamia.

Maybe tomorrow morning he didn't need a jog around Circular Quay or a pistachio–almond croissant in Glebe. Maybe what he needed was God. Or at least a community to grieve with. He could do with a stock-up of spices from the grocer on Haldon Street, too.

It had been years since Ashraf had been to Heartlands, and the last time was neither for prayer nor for communal celebration but for his uncle's burial service. This time it took him almost half an hour of scouting to find a parking spot in the side streets around York Road. Eventually he squeezed his red BMW behind a beat-up Corolla in front of a brown-brick bungalow. The front porch was cluttered with plastic toys and portable washing lines, and somebody had made a slide with an old mattress and broken cot in the front yard.

There were Muslims everywhere, from everywhere, walking in the direction of the mosque. He followed a family, Indian background was his guess, and listened to the boy and girl arguing about whether they would watch *Jurassic Park 2* or *Jurassic Park 3* for movie night that evening.

The crowd surged as they got closer to the mosque, the out-of-tune sound of the congregation chanting *Labayk Allah* streaming from the mosque speaker system. He found himself behind a group of young hijabis, probably in their twenties. It was an odd mix. One of them was niqabi. Another wore a hijab wrapped tightly around her head over a long, loose dress. Another wore a turban, short tight top that hugged her chest and skin-tight skirt that showed off her arse. Mya would have been incensed (not just about the 'unIslamic dress' but also the fact he was perving on a hijabi girl half his age in front of a mosque).

Ashraf entered the mosque with the wudu ablution he performed at home (though it had been a while since he had done one).

He no longer cared much for the ritual of prayer. He had enjoyed a fairly solid run as a devout and devoted religious nut job as a young teenager. Intoxicated by Wahhabi pamphlets freely distributed at the Arabic school his parents had sent him to in the early nineties, he would stay up for hours at night, acne-riddled face in prostration, begging God to save him from hellfire. His father would have to coax him into bed and reassure him that God cared about his character more than He cared about him forgetting to enter the toilet with his left foot.

Prayer to him now was like a long-forgotten love interest. Once upon a time it had filled his life, given him moments of euphoria and purpose. And then one day, like an adolescent crush, the feeling switched off. It aroused nothing in him.

He went through the motions next to a smiling old Afghan man with a walnut-brown face and a beefed-up twenty-something with two sleeve tattoos, Prada bum bag and garlic breath (probably a reformed gangster or Ramadan Muslim).

When the prayer was finished, they sat down, crossed their legs and buckled up for the khutba.

It was a fiery one.

'Gaza is being bombed because Arab life is cheap, Muslim life is cheap. We expect this from Western countries, but where is the Muslim world? God doesn't help people until they help themselves. The condition of the ummah is the test!'

It was a perplexing sermon, a masterclass in how to speak to multiple audiences and end up confusing everyone. It was a patchwork quilt: a patch of anti-imperialism, a patch of Aussie, good-migrant patriotism, a patch of ummah philosophy, a patch of guilt tripping (you miss your prayers, you are miserly with your wealth, Gaza bleeds), a patch of Islamic history.

Ashraf wanted it over and done with so he could see Fayza and Hasan, grab a fresh zaatar man'oushe and restock his spice cupboard. But then the imam launched into a tirade about Muslim youth.

'They see the injustice, they see people who look like them being bombed in their homes, and we give them no solutions! No outlet! But it's the youf who have everything to lose! Whose names were splashed across the media after that group was arrested at the university? Was it those of the non-Muslims? No! The system is designed to lock up our youf! It was the Muslim boy who was painted as the evil mastermind. He was pushed to Marx, not the Quran! Where were the adults and teachers in his life? The Islamic school that didn't guide him? Where is the duty to protect our youf from themselves? This is a system that will sacrifice them for politics.'

Knowing that the sermons were always monitored by police didn't render the experience of listening to one so discombobulating and convoluted any less unpleasant, and Ashraf regretted attending.

He tried to distract himself with his phone. Tattoo guy next to him had the same idea and was scrolling through TikTok. Ashraf's phone showed a message from Fayza.

Can you believe this nonsense?! I want to leave straight after prayer. I've told Hasan I'll meet you both outside. Driveway, next door.

When at last the imam had finished, the congregation rose to pray.

After prayer, Ashraf followed in the wake of the tattooed bouncer rather than the small Afghan and was pushed by the flow of people outside, down the side stairway to the shoe section. He found his shoes only to then be pushed again by the throng moving towards the bottom of the mosque's front steps.

On the way down, Ashraf noticed that microphones had been set up on the platform at the top of the mosque's stairs. Standing there was the NSW premier flanked by a few ethnic members of parliament, (male) representatives of the mosque board and three uniformed AFP officers. Reporters and camera crews from the state's main news channels were there to cover the spectacle. A short, bearded man in a slightly oversized suit stepped up to the podium. Ashraf recognised him as Shahid Kazi – he'd been the president of the mosque board for over fifteen years

In a broad Australian accent, Kazi spoke proudly about the Muslim community 'contributing to the growth and prosperity of New South Wales and the big Australian family'. He lamented 'the humanitarian disaster our brothers and sisters are going through' and urged the 'need to pray for them'. He then praised Australia's 'status as the most multicultural and most multi-faith country in the world'.

Ashraf understood this was all a performance, the calculated logic of realpolitik. Claiming a 'seat at the table' and so on. It rested on the delusion that such engagements were symbiotic, even mutually beneficial, as though it was the community and not the politicians who benefited from being handed a platform on which to deliver speeches. It was a parasitic relationship that ignored the power differential.

But Ashraf was an academic, and he had no shame conceding that he was in the business of interpreting and analysing, not of solving or agitating. He wouldn't judge those who worked at the coalface of community and politics and, anyway, he was not so naive as to expect Muslim civic organisations and mosque boards to be bastions of radical, decolonial, anti-racist, anti-capitalist and feminist politics. (It would be a good thing if they could start with a woman on their board.)

He was tired and overstimulated, and he'd had enough. He tried to edge his way out of the crowd as the premier took to the podium. Behind a large green Muslim Association Organisation banner, he delivered a Wikipedia-standard reflection on the meaning of Ramadan ('This is a time in which Muslims fast from sunrise to sunset; a month of spiritual reflection' et cetera) and then reminded the crowd of hundreds that in 'a world of conflict, pain and hardship we must embrace our shared humanity'.

It was at that point that Ashraf noticed a commotion towards the side of the mosque. At first it was just indecipherable shouting. And then he picked up a steady chant of 'Free Free Palestine!'

The camera crew, like sharks to blood, barrelled towards the protesters. The reporters looked giddy with excitement. They'd scored the premier at Eid prayers *and* a juicy disturbance.

Police officers and security guards charged at the protesters, escorting them away from the crowd towards the car park, and that is when Ashraf noticed Jamal among them. Instinctively he rushed over.

Jamal, two more young men and two young women, none of whom he recognised, were standing against a brick wall surrounded by police officers. Ashraf approached with caution, cleared his throat and, with appropriate deference, interrupted. He explained that Jamal was his student, that he could vouch for him, and asked if he could help.

Jamal was defiant. 'This is a sacred space,' he kept saying, calmly. 'Those politicians should not be here.'

'Step away, sir,' a police officer said to Ashraf.

'But I can help. I'm working with this student on his PhD.'

Jamal and his companion remained surrounded.

'Sir, I've asked you to step away,' the officer repeated politely but firmly.

Ashraf stood to the side and texted Fayza and Hasan to tell them where he was. He wouldn't leave until he knew Jamal was safe.

Fayza and Hasan found Ashraf and waited with him. A young woman with a baby – Jamal's family, he assumed – appeared at the scene and started pleading with the police to let Jamal go.

Fayza pointed to the woman, saying that she recognised her as a journalist who had visited the school fishing for a story. Ashraf explained that he doubted, given Jamal was her partner, she was that kind of journalist, although one never could tell.

Soon, Jamal was allowed to leave. His wife hurried towards him and pulled him away. Jamal waved at Ashraf as he walked off with her, holding his baby.

The crowds slowly dispersed, the politicians posed for photos with mosque board members, Muslim babies and beaming hijabis, and Ashraf ended the morning with a zaatar man'oushe, a terrible headache and no spices.

20

It was Hannah's day off and she was in bed, scrolling on her phone, switching between Twitter, Instagram and TikTok. Aya sat nestled in her walker at the foot of the bed, playing with the tray of colourful built-in toys.

Somebody, many people, had posted a video of the imam's khutba online. Somebody else, and many others, posted a video of the Free Palestine protest and the police breaking it up.

The Muslim Association Organisation Facebook page posted a video of the state premier delivering his speech alongside a collage of photos with community figures. A rival – the Islamic Organisation Association – posted a press release condemning the protests as inappropriate. A rival of *that* organisation – the Muslim Community Collective Organisation – posted tiles on Instagram criticising the Muslim Association Organisation, not only for inviting politicians at a time when Gaza was being bombed but also for inviting the premier to supposedly 'celebrate' the Muslim community with photo-ops on the mosque steps, when only last week he'd whipped up fear and suspicion about Islamic schools and 'radicalisation'.

The media was in a frenzy. *Imam's Eid Message: Give Muslim kids the Koran not Marx. Eid at Heartlands Marred by Protests and Fears for Muslim Youth. NSW Premier Attacked by Gaza Mosque Protesters. Israel–Hamas War Comes to Sydney Mosque.*

Hannah set down her phone on the bedside table and jumped out of bed. She needed fresh air, exercise. She decided to go for a walk around the track at the park near her house. She dressed, packed a bag of snacks and toys to entertain Aya in the pram, and set out.

Post-Eid hydrated with two decaf coffees and a Gatorade, Hannah kept up a brisk pace pushing the pram around Campbell Hill Park as she listened to a podcast on getting into shape after a baby. Aya was playing with a musical toy in the pram and making happy noises at the birds flying above and every dog they passed on the path.

Hannah's phone rang. It was Jeanette. She knew she had to take the call. Jeanette was strictly a text person. Heck, most of them were so overstimulated and fatigued that to place an actual phone call meant serious business. She answered.

'We need to go live with the open letter,' Jeanette said breathlessly. 'They're going to shift the attention away from bombs on Gaza with a Muslim-kids-are-being-radicalised-and-pro-Palestine-protestors-are-violent propaganda job.'

'Yeah, I know,' Hannah agreed. 'It's bullshit journalism.' They both felt now, amid the media circus, was as suitable a time as any to publish. They were discussing the content of social media assets and who would collaborate on the posts when a text message from Jamal appeared on Hannah's phone. 'Hang on,' she said to Jeanette. She slowed down to read the text, pausing to hand Aya, who was starting to fuss, an apricot finger bar.

They published a story beside yours, Jamal's text read. *Profiles a Jewish doctor from Randwick whose son is in Israel. He's terrified for his son and his son's family in their shelter. Oh, and their scared dog.*

Hannah opened the link Jamal sent with his text, bracing herself. The story, headline *Hamas Rockets Traumatise Australian Jewish Families*, was under Peter's byline. Her tongue suddenly felt dry, like it would disintegrate into ash.

She scrolled down and read the article, stopping at a photograph of a man and woman smiling into the camera as they hugged a large German Shepherd. The caption: *Ittay and Ramona with their beloved dog Charlie.* At the bottom of the article was a 'Read more' section and a link to her article: *'Painful and so unfair': Palestinian Australians celebrate a sombre Eid.*

'What the hell?' she said.

'You okay?' Jeanette asked.

Hannah filled her in as she jogged the pram to the closest bench and sat down on.

‘I’m so sorry, Hannah,’ Jeanette said.

They ended the call as a notification popped up on the WhatsApp organising group from Rima, whose parents were in Gaza, sharing a dispatch from the Palestinian Ministry of Health: *Gaza update – 119 Palestinians killed including 31 children and 19 women, while 830 were wounded as a result of the ongoing Israeli airstrikes on the Gaza Strip.*

Hannah started typing a response with one hand as she rocked the pram back and forth with the other to stop Aya crying every time the pram stood motionless.

As she was typing she received another text from Jamal, who had forwarded a message from his mother: *Last night was the most barbaric shelling anyone could ever imagine. Non-stop bombardments and explosions. Children and even adults are terrified, shaking and crying. May Allah bless Gaza and its people.*

Aya suddenly hated the confines of the pram and started trying to claw her way out.

Hannah closed her eyes and squeezed the bridge of her nose as she surrendered to self-pity. Gaza was being bombed and her plans for a one-hour power walk were ruined.

This was what her life had been reduced to. The grotesque and the banal all folded into one another so that everything was inflected with existential meaning.

She needed this walk: because the oppressor thrived on her burnout; because her thighs were proof she’d eaten too many acai bowls during pregnancy, and if she couldn’t stop the bombs at least she could lose weight; because she needed an exercise-induced endorphin hit; because she couldn't afford therapy. She was on the verge of crying. It was like this at some point almost every day now.

Her mother, Donya, had counselled her the other night at iftar, after Hannah had snapped at Jamal for forgetting to pack spare clothes in Aya's bag: 'I'm worried about you. You're so tense, so wound up,' to which Hannah, incredulous, had shot back, 'Do you expect me to be calm at such a time?' knowing, as she said this, that it was unfair of her to suggest that her parents – refugees, for goodness sake – were unaffected.

They lived with the debris of Nakba in their lives every single day but had learnt to train their bodies and minds not to dwell on the piles of trauma, fear and anxiety. They had cultivated a way of living in which, especially when surrounded by family, they swept the debris into the background.

Donya had pulled her aside into the spare bedroom and ordered her to sit down on the edge of the bed.

Hannah, reduced to a teenager by one withering look from her Arab mother, had plopped down obediently.

'Aren't we all turned inside out?' Donya had said, scrunching her fist against her chest. 'Ya Allah, the scenes last night! Your father and I were watching the news for hours. But there must be limits! You're not helping them by hurting yourself. You must look after yourself.'

Hannah had shaken her head and let out a long sigh. 'I'm not doing this just for *them*. I'm doing it for Aya. If we don't, what will be left of our land? What will be left for Aya to return to?'

'But it's affecting you too much.'

'Being affected by what's happening *is* looking after myself! Grief is love. At least my heart is alive. It's the people who don't feel a thing that you should worry about.'

'You have a baby, Hannah,' Donya had gently scolded her. 'You're breastfeeding. All that stress and negative energy is affecting you *and* Aya.'

'How do I raise a Palestinian child while they're killing Palestinian children, Mum? Do you expect me to switch off?' And then she had burst into tears.

Donya had held her close, allowing her an ugly, snotty cry against her chest, while she proceeded to counsel Hannah about self-care.

Hannah had pretended to listen and falsely promised to heed Donya's clichéd fill-your-cup, do-Pilates-or-yoga, you-can't-run-on-empty advice. She *loathed* such advice.

Hannah took a deep breath. She unbuckled Aya's seatbelt, took her out of the pram, propped her up on her hip, kissed her cheek and began pushing the pram back to the house with one hand. Aya fidgeted against her body, trying to escape. Hannah lost her temper and cried out at Aya: 'Just stop!'

Aya began to cry and Hannah felt disgusted with herself.

It was a slow journey back. She had to stop a few times to shift Aya from hip to hip, tickling her, trying but always failing to put her back into the pram, before finally they arrived home.

21

Ashraf was deep in university admin hell, finally uploading a reimbursement claim for his Melbourne conference, when Jamal barged into his office wanting to discuss an email he'd received from a journalist at *The Daily Current*, Jessica Heaton. Ashraf had never seen Jamal in such an agitated state.

Jamal paced Ashraf's office as he read the email aloud: '"You are a PhD student at JBU and you were involved in a pro-Palestine protest at Heartlands Mosque. Do you have any connection with Nabil Mostafa, a Hamas supporter who occupied a building at JBU?" What kind of ridiculous assumption is that?' Jamal spat. 'She goes on: "You recently shared, to your LinkedIn account, a video by Weapons of Mass Interruption of their occupation of the JBU building, adding the comment: *Heroes*. Do you condone the actions of Weapons of Mass Interruption?" Yes, I do!'

'You can't say that,' Ashraf said in a panic.

Jamal rolled his eyes. 'I'm not going to *say* anything to this trash, obviously. This next question, somebody leaked my email, listen: “You recently circulated an unauthorised statement for Palestine to JBU staff—” *Unauthorised!* See how they twist everything? “—causing some staff distress.” Oh, I’m sorry you were distressed about a statement, but they’re wiping entire families off the Gaza population registry. And then, check this out, they want me to respond to a quote by the CEO of the Zionist Executive Association of Australia. What on earth is this orchestrated, malicious campaign?’

Leigh walked past, saw Jamal and backed up. She locked eyes with Ashraf.

He nodded and Leigh entered, closing the door behind her. Ashraf motioned for Leigh to take the seat next to a side table, and Jamal sat on the wide window ledge looking at them both nervously.

Ashraf quickly spoke to forestall Jamal’s concern, and suggested Jamal update Leigh on the media request. ‘Let’s put our heads together and see how to de-escalate this.’

Jamal gave Leigh an account of the journalist’s email.

Leigh nodded along, listening intently. When Jamal finished explaining she reassured him that she appreciated he was going through a difficult time and that ‘emotions were running high’.

She was soft-spoken and Ashraf had no reason to suspect she was here out of anything but genuine concern for Jamal and yet, to Ashraf’s consternation, Jamal sat stiff and tight-lipped.

‘It’s your decision, of course,’ Leigh said, ‘but in my view, it’s best not to respond. I suspect they already have their story and angle and nothing you say will change that.’

‘I have no intention of responding,’ Jamal said calmly.

Suddenly his phone loudly called out ‘Allahu Akbar’, the Athan app signalling it was time for the midday prayer. Jamal silenced it, but Ashraf noticed Leigh’s slight flinch.

‘This conflict between Israel and Hamas—’

‘Actually, I must correct you there, Leigh,’ interrupted Jamal. ‘It’s not a conflict but an occupation and apartheid, and it’s not between Israel and Hamas.’

‘Yes, well, um, Jamal. I understand this is a complex matter and there are multiple articulations. The thing to try to appreciate, Jamal, is that this issue generates passionate engagement.’ Leigh was evading Jamal’s gaze, looking at Ashraf or the ground as she spoke. ‘While you may think you’re approaching this in a moderate and sensitive way, others with equally passionate views may not find your engagement as, er, moderate. We need to learn how to strike that balance. I’m not trying to tell you how to speak. But speaking as an academic attached to a university and therefore subject to its policies means there are considerations.’

‘Such as?’

‘Take your social media. There’s a post on there. The student is being charged with a terrorism offence and yet in one of your posts you publicly call him a hero, supporting him. That’s a very risky position to take.’

'How so?'

Leigh reflected, hesitating for a moment. 'It suggests you support Hamas.'

'What does that – *support Hamas* – even mean?' Jamal asked.

Leigh looked taken aback.

Ashraf cleared his throat nervously.

Jamal didn't give either a chance to respond. 'Do you mean have I provided material support?' he asked. 'No. Do I fundraise or advocate on their behalf as an organisation? No. Do I represent them legally or diplomatically? No. What you and everyone else disconnected from the daily reality of life as a Palestinian want to know is: "Do you, in your heart of hearts, hate Hamas the way the state has determined you must hate them?" I mean, it's the clearest possible example of prosecuting a thought crime.'

'That's not … what I …'

Jamal took advantage of her trailing voice and cut her off: 'Ultimately, it's a question of academic freedom, isn't it?' He clasped his hands together under his chin.

'Yes, of course,' Leigh said curtly. 'Universities are spaces of intellectual challenge and the contest of ideas. But …'

'But?'

'They must never be places of hate speech or intimidation. Not that I'm suggesting that you engage in such speech. I'm just reminding us of the curves and contours of our speech acts. Rights are never absolute.'

'True,' Ashraf said in the background.

Jamal was regarding Leigh with an impenetrable stare.

'The key,' Leigh continued, in a sympathetic tone, 'is to find a way to be *careful* in how we engage in healthy intellectual debate and be mindful of not crossing certain lines.'

Jamal smiled wryly. 'Is it curves or lines?'

Leigh blinked. 'Pardon?'

'I'm just trying to grasp which metaphor I should apply to my academic freedom as a Palestinian.'

Leigh looked uncomfortable and Ashraf felt sorry for her.

'Sorry, that was a bit muddled,' she said with a half-laugh and the look of somebody who would rather be doing anything else.

22

Hannah stood among a sea of people gathered around Sydney's Town Hall in the CBD. Two loud choppers circled overhead.

The protest organisers had put on a performance in front of the stage in Hyde Park. Dolls of babies and children wrapped in 'bloodied' (red-painted) shrouds were placed on the ground. Protesters of all ages and backgrounds, faces and clothes smeared in red, stood vigil over the bodies. Linda Tanning, an Aboriginal activist, delivered a fierce, stunning speech: 'Australia is a crime scene,' she roared to thunderous applause. People were recording Linda's speech and the die-in on their phones, streaming live on Instagram and TikTok.

Hannah took photos of the placards around her. Several referenced *73 Years of Nakba!* A young man in Nike TNs with a bun and a thick black beard stood nearby holding a placard with a drawing of the incredible hulk, caption: *Even Hulk says 'Free Palestine'.* His friend, standing and laughing beside him, held up a sign that read, *Israel is like my love life:*

Non-existent. A woman holding a baby against her chest in a swaddle held up a placard, *From the River to the Sea, Always Was Always Will Be.*

A young Palestinian organiser, Yasmeen, stepped up to the microphone. A bandana in the colours of the Palestine flag held her mane of curly hair back from her face.

'Where is the media?' she asked. 'I can see an ABC crew is here today. Why don't you do your job? Israel just bombed a building where families lived. That building housed the offices of international media outlets: Associated Press, *Al Jazeera*, BBC and *Middle East Eye*! The footage is devastating. This is a direct attack on press freedom! This is an attempt to kill the messengers and witnesses! But what was the ABC's headline?'

Yasmeen paused as the crowd booed. Then she pressed on.

'"Israeli Forces Destroy Media Outlets' Gaza Base, Says It Housed Hamas Military Intelligence". Is the ABC our national broadcaster or Israel's PR stenographer?'

It was like every word Yasmeen uttered fed a raging furnace. The crowd roared: 'Shame!'

A news update flashed on Hannah's phone: *Gaza death toll nears 200 amid surge of Israeli raids.* She read on: *Israeli air raids on Gaza City flatten three buildings and kill at least 42 people on Sunday.*

Hannah forced herself to hold these figures in her mind as she wondered who gets counted and who gets lost in the dehumanising game of approximation? Who becomes a carry-the-one, a remainder in the maths of slaughter that drops bombs so that a whole body cannot be counted? How do you count a whole body when it's been torn into unidentifiable parts and limbs?

Yasmeen concluded her speech and introduced Jamal.

The crowd clapped and cheered as he stepped forward in front of the microphone, his *Zionism is Fascism* t-shirt on display. His eyes searched for and then locked with Hannah's. She placed her palm firmly over her heart.

'I'm a PhD student at JBU, the same university where a high school student was recently arrested for occupying a university building in protest at my institution's ties with weapons manufacturer Elbit Systems.'

Jamal paused, interrupted by the crowd screaming, 'Shame!'

'I stand in solidarity with Nabil,' he bellowed, 'and with those brave young activists who put their bodies on the line! With fifty-one per cent of Gaza's population under the age of fifteen, a war on Gaza is a war on children. I'm disgusted by JBU, a university that revels in holding conferences, seminars and talkfests about genocide, violence, settler colonialism, decolonisation and social movements but has absolutely no moral issue with its relationships with weapons manufacturers and other companies with ties to Israel's military!'

The cry of 'shame' once again reverberated through the crowd.

'JBU's message to students is clear: study genocide, but don't dare protest it. Write about genocide, but don't dare question our complicity in it.'

The crowd erupted in applause.

'I was born and lived most of my life in Gaza,' Jamal continued. 'This didn't start with Hamas rockets. This didn't start with the attacks on Al Aqsa. This didn't start with the Zionist squatters in Sheikh Jarrah. This is seventy-three years of colonisation and brutal apartheid against the indigenous people of the land of Palestine. When Israel's bombs over Gaza stop, the world will reset. It'll keep on ignoring Israel's slow genocide. The slow death caused by the siege, the occupation, the colonisation of land and resources, "mowing the lawn", Dahiya doctrine, red lines and calorie controlling, calls to "flatten", to "wipe out", to "finish us". So I say nothing less than the end to the Zionist state and a free Palestine of equals, from the river to the sea!'

Shouts and whoops echoed through the audience.

As Jamal stepped off the stage, Hannah saw a woman approach him. She immediately recognised her as Jessica Heaton, the reporter from *The Daily Current* who'd emailed him about what happened at Heartlands Mosque. Hannah rushed to his side to warn him, but was too late.

Jessica was shoving a phone in Jamal's face: 'Do you support students breaking the law to protest Israel? Do you condemn Hamas? Do you know Nabil?'

'Just fuck off, will you!' Hannah yelled at Jessica.

Jessica looked outraged.

Jamal stood calm and composed. He stared Jessica down, refusing to respond. Then he gently took Hannah's hand and led her away.

The front doorbell rang at 5 o'clock. Hannah and Jamal's half-Maltese, half-Lebanese neighbour Simone stood on their porch with a letter from state debt recovery, asking for help. George, her twenty-nine-year-old son, was an unsuccessful drug dealer ('Ya Adra! Everything he does he fails at!') and was deep in debt. He had absconded to Lebanon and Simone was worried the government would come after her house.

Hannah explained the letter and reassured Simone that she wasn't liable for George's debts, sparking a stream of blessings and the sign of the cross from Simone.

Hannah closed the door and rushed back to Jamal, who was sitting on the lounge watching the news. As she recounted the story, the two of them collapsed into a fit of giggles.

Aya, propped up against pillows between them, chewing on a teething ring, started mimicking them and giggling.

Hannah's phone pinged with a notification from Rima on the media chat group. It was a link to Jessica's article and the message: *WTF.*

They read it together on Hannah's phone.

Anti-Israel PhD Scholarship Student Praises School Student Arrested on Anti-terror Laws

This afternoon, Jamal Abdul-Hamid, who was born in the Hamas-controlled Gaza strip, wore a t-shirt that read 'Zionism is Fascism' to address a crowd of pro-Palestine protesters in Sydney's CBD, where people, including families with their children, chanted controversial anti-Israel slogans such as 'From the river to the sea Palestine will be free' and 'intifada, intifada'.

The slogan 'From the river to the sea Palestine will be free' is understood to be a call for the destruction of Israel.

In the context of the Palestine–Israel conflict, the term 'intifada' is often associated with Palestinian violent resistance.

Mr Abdul-Hamid lashed the university and accused it of being 'complicit in war crimes' through its alleged contracts with 'weapons manufacturers and other companies with ties to Israel's military'.

Mr Abdul-Hamid advocated for the destruction of Israel, ending his speech with a call to 'end the Zionist state', attracting huge applause from the crowd.

At Joseph Banks University on a three-year PhD scholarship in the Department of Politics, where he teaches subjects including 'Introduction to Global Politics' to first-year students, Mr Abdul-Hamid is no stranger to controversy and was at the centre of a flash protest at Heartlands Mosque on 13 May, which some Muslim congregants on the mosque's Facebook page condemned as 'divisive' and 'ruining the Eid spirit'.

In his speech at the CBD rally, Mr Abdul-Hamid praised the Weapons of Mass Interruption occupation of JBU on 5 May and sent a 'shout-out' to 18-year-old Nabil Mostafa, who was arrested on terror charges following the illegal occupation.

Mr Abdul-Hamid shared a link to the livestream of the Weapons of Mass Interruption occupation with the comment 'Heroes' on his LinkedIn profile.

It is not suggested that Mr Abdul-Hamid knows Nabil Mostafa or that he has any association with Weapons of Mass Interruption or that he had any involvement in the JBU occupation operation.

However, Mr Abdul-Hamid declined to respond to questions when approached after the rally.

Zionist Executive Association of Australia CEO Ari Meir expressed disappointment, stating: 'At a time of cuts to higher education, PhD scholarships are ever more competitive.

'It is therefore alarming to see students in higher degree research who engage in hate speech and antisemitism receive funding.

'This is a direct threat to multiculturalism and social cohesion at a time when antisemitism is increasing.'

Jamal immediately opened his email on his phone. 'I need to send it to Ashraf and Leigh,' he told Hannah. 'Send them my version of events before they read it and panic.'

'But how do you even respond to this garbage?' Hannah asked angrily.

She shook a rattle to distract Aya, who had started fussing in response to her raised voice.

'Every line is a set-up of plausible deniability and innuendo. I mean, what if you did know Nabil? What if you were associated with Weapons of Mass Interruption? So fucking what? Your email to Leigh and Ashraf can't be defensive. You can't dignify any of it. I'm going to ask Jeanette to do some Insta tiles, like a primer on intifada and maybe a video or factsheet on "from the river to the sea",' she said, bashing out a message on her phone. 'Their fucking existential crisis. Their projection makes me want to puke.'

Jamal gave Hannah a pointed look. 'Aya's first word is actually going to be the f-word,' he said.

'Relax,' Hannah countered. 'I'm sure some academic has written some paper about how the f-word is a social construct. You're the one who told me about that Sokal guy who published a whole hoax article arguing gravity is a social and linguistic construct to expose how self-indulgent academia can be.'

'Hannah,' he said, shaking his head. 'What's that got to do with you dropping f-bombs?'

Hannah grinned. 'Okay, okay, I promise I'll try harder. They go low, we go high, BS, BS. Yalla, let's write the email.'

There were a few emails at the top of Jamal's inbox with charming subject lines such as *You're a grifting Islamo-fascist Pally-nazi propagandist* and *Fuck off back to Hamasistan.*

'See, I'm not the only one with an f-bomb problem,' Hannah joked, squeezing Jamal's arm affectionately.

They composed a simple email to Ashraf and Leigh, attaching the 'incendiary article'.

Leigh replied within the hour.

Dear Jamal,

Thank you for bringing the article to my attention. I hope it is not exacerbating your stress in difficult times.

Please remember the JBU Wellbeing app offers resources on wellbeing and stress management.

Kind regards,
Leigh

23

Ashraf had no classes on Monday, so he'd decided to work from home. He was deep in background reading for his new project and the more he read on radicalisation and extremism the more ashamed he felt. He'd failed his daughters because he'd failed his wife. He'd failed to notice the warning signs – the gradual detachment from her lifestyle, her gradual rejection of what had been a normal part of their lives for years.

Voraciously, hungrily, he read the academic research that experts had dedicated their careers to producing. There was the case of Mohammad Sidique Khan. Reports described him as a previously 'easygoing guy' to someone who became 'more introverted and intolerant'. According to the report, 'Khan's new religious practices and attitude caused conflict with the family and his life became intensely narrow and confined to the mosques where he prayed, the buildings where he helped run youth groups, the bookshop where he gave talks and his brother's house'. It was like reading Mya's trajectory.

There was also the case of Tamerlan Tsarnaev. He'd 'renounced boxing as an offence against Islam'. Mya had given up bike-riding. Tsarnaev had 'gone from being cocky' and 'wearing leather shoes and white shirts to the gym, to growing a five-inch beard and dressing conservatively'. Mya had been bubbly and outgoing, and her formerly glamorous style had been subsumed by shapeless maxi dresses in muted, block colours. Tsarnaev also stopped listening to rap music and playing the piano and violin. Mya had replaced music with nasheeds.

She'd replaced alcohol with soft drinks, then soft drinks with juice or water when she decided to boycott Coke and Pepsi (because the entire Israeli occupation would collapse if she stopped having a Coke at dinner). After that it was praying, even if they were out – she would pray in car parks, shopping-centre change rooms. And fasting. And then there was the dreaded day, the day he knew was coming, when he woke up to find her dressed for work, her luscious curls covered in a hijab.

Ashraf was intelligent enough to understand that he was engaged in an exercise of hindsight, assembling independent actions into a coherent chain, reconstructing Mya's 'warning signs' after the fact. In a way, he was working backwards to prove the outcome he was now compelled to live with.

But he could see now that radicalisation was a virus and that he had failed to pick up the symptoms. Much as running a fever, sneezing or having body aches is to cold and flu,

Mya had been clearly symptomatic, vulnerable and at risk in her feverish rejection of a life she had once cherished and valued. And who had she exposed? Who had she infected with a virus that had already taken what was pure and joyful and loving in their lives and imbued it with corrupt, foul meaning? Their daughters.

He was furious, he was funded and he felt he had finally found a means of redemption.

There was a knock on the door and he realised the whole morning had passed. Chantelle had arrived to clean.

While Chantelle was working, Ashraf took himself to the onsite gym that his exorbitant strata fees subsidised. He had always kept fit and active – even more so, with so much time on his hands, following the divorce.

The gym wasn't too busy, and he settled in for a leg workout, putting on his headphones and ramping up the volume on his 2000s dance music Spotify playlist in an effort to muffle the sound of the oversized guy beside him who was making weird noises with every chest press.

After an intense set, he wiped down the leg press machine and stepped aside as a serious-looking woman, dressed head-to-toe in hot-pink, took over.

He chugged back some water and stretched in front of the mirrors, his eyes wandering around the small gym floor. The news was playing on a TV mounted above the treadmills. He hadn't noticed that the sound, usually muted, was audible. A woman had been arrested in Lakemba for burning an Israeli flag during a protest. The prime minister was at a press conference in Canberra: 'Israel has the right to defend itself and we will always remain one of Israel's truest friends and support a two-state solution. We support people's right to protest but people shouldn't import the Middle East conflict to Australia. We need to ensure people live in this country with tolerance and respect.'

Figuring that Chantelle would be finished by now, Ashraf decided to head back upstairs. He was in a pensive mood and, as he exited the elevator, he wondered about the madness of it all.

Nobody in the gym had shown the slightest curiosity in the news. So much suffering and violence, but it was just background noise to them. When Lebanon was being bombed by Israel in 2006, there were times he wondered why people didn't pause everything to demand the bombing stop and for Australia to sanction Israel.

But really, like now with Gaza, why would they? He didn't begrudge anybody their apathy. He understood it. He had left his Marxist days long behind him, but he did still understand that capitalism had trapped everyone in the world into a tightly wound ball of string. Pull a thread in one spot, and while you might loosen the grip for some people, you would tighten things for others down the line. People had to look out for themselves.

Ashraf stepped inside his apartment.

Chantelle was packing her bag, and she greeted him with her usual deference, avoiding eye contact. He smiled at her, tried to put her at ease. He hated these hierarchies.

He wanted to ask her how her studies were going, how she was surviving the juggling act. He knew she was studying and working round the clock: domestic cleaning jobs and nights at a restaurant in Ultimo – small scraps of information via text when they were working out schedules. But her English was too limited for the two of them to engage in any small talk.

He handed her the cash and, because Gaza was burning and the world was fucked, gave her a little extra.

She thanked him and left.

Ashraf showered, still consumed by the scale of injustice and horror in the world. People like Jamal and these flag-burning protesters were delusional if they didn't comprehend that their moral absolutism only resonated with their echo chamber of keyboard warriors and angry rent-a-crowds.

That's why their movements – and yes, even those movements that had demanded the end of Israel's bombing of Lebanon in 2006 – were doomed to fail. They didn't understand that, because everyone was so tightly bound in that societal ball of string and struggling to survive, they couldn't afford to fight for others. What could Chantelle, struggling with uni fees, cash-in-hand jobs, shitty bosses (self excluded), crappy public transport, seven dollars for a kilo of almost-expired Aldi cucumbers and a bastard of a landlord, do for Mohammed from Nablus, who was being shot at by a settler, or for Diyana, whose Beirut apartment building was being bombed?

The world was selfish, ugly, unjust and expensive to live in. Free Palestine, sure, but nothing in this world was for free, so who would pay the price?

To reckon with the global was an exercise in futility and despair. The only choice was to focus on the local.

Ashraf sat down to eat leftover Thai for a late lunch. He'd left his phone on the charger in his bedroom since the morning and had been grateful for the break. Bracing himself for an avalanche of notifications, he unlocked his phone and saw that he'd missed an email from Jamal overnight. It was addressed to him and Leigh and shared a link to an article.

He read the article straight through. It was only when he finished that he realised he'd practically been holding his breath.

Jamal had become a liability. Here was an article in a paper, a national paper, insinuating that Jamal, his PhD student Jamal, was connected with Nabil – Nabil, who had been arrested and embroiled in a radicalisation scandal.

Jamal's name was in the ethics application and project proposal. He would have to fix that. Ashraf's name was in Jamal's email signature too. He would have to ask him to remove it. He needed to distance himself as much as he could. Was it possible to withdraw as his supervisor? He would investigate.

There were other people in the department who had just as much to offer Jamal as he did. It's not as though he was the only suitable supervisor. There was Brendan, for instance. His Arabic was shocking but he got points for trying. And Faye 'Loves Bedouins' Nickel. At least neither would be hostile.

It suddenly dawned on him that his project proposal relied on participants recruited by Jamal. That was now – thanks to Jamal's stupid, self-indulgent virtue signalling and belief that one could be an academic and an activist – completely untenable.

He was back at square one.

As he threw away his takeaway packaging and wiped down the kitchen counter, he racked his brain for a recruitment strategy. Who did he know who had access to young Muslims?

The solution had been there all along. He couldn't believe he hadn't thought of it at the start.

24

Hannah was deep in a heated argument on the WhatsApp organising group about the Nakba rally promotional poster. The poster featured a black-and-white photo of young men with keffiyehs tied around their heads and faces throwing stones.

Nader had sent it to the group and said: *Getting feedback this isn't the best photo to mobilise non-Palestinians for the protest. Thoughts?*

Hannah was unimpressed with the question. She responded: *Looks like an intifada pic. I think it's fine.*

Jeanette agreed: *If people don't want to attend because of this photo, then are they the people we want standing with us? That's just my take. I'm sure others have more diplomatic insights.*

Danny jumped in: *We need to win more people to our cause, as frustrating as it is to tone-police our movement.*

Rima was not impressed: *It's resistance to violence!*

Mikael suddenly popped up: *Is it promoting violence? Perception.*

Hannah was incensed.

Jeanette responded to Mikael with an angry emoji and said: *Perception is one thing, but the reality is Gaza is being BOMBED. Why should we deny the right to resist at the very moment we should be asserting it?*

Hannah added a love heart to Jeanette's comment and said: *I really don't care what white people think. And how it fits their sensibilities. I'm sick of people denying our right to resist. We need to stand up for ourselves and our rights.*

Danny, who often played the role of mediator, sent a message in a clear attempt to divert the conversation: *Did you see Newsweek calling on people to 'give war a chance'? Check this out: 'The cost of the war must be so great that Hamas will not be able to repeat its periodic foray of violence ... If the dog is to survive, then the fleas must be destroyed in their earliest stages.'*

Hannah blanched and replied: *We're at the Palestinians-are-fleas stage of the war.*

Before she knew it, forty-five minutes – of banter, serious discussion, coordinating the next round of calls to action, delegating interview requests and arguing over how to strategise in response to an imminent trade and investment deal between Australia and Israel – had passed. It was close to midnight and she was going cross-eyed.

Jamal was still up too but had muted the WhatsApp group to instead obsessively read updates from Arabic media and tweet furiously.

Aya started crying.

Jamal rose to go to her, but Hannah stopped him and went instead. Aya was what she needed right now.

It hit Hannah as she was rocking Aya to sleep: *Time is running out.*

She had hoped, last year, to visit Palestine with her parents. It would have been a pilgrimage of return to their family homes – albeit on their Australian passports, as tourists in their homeland and with an enforced exit date on their visas.

When she had fallen pregnant and their travel plans were postponed, her father Mansoor confessed to her one evening as they ate fetta and watermelon in the backyard and he smoked his argeela that he was relieved.

Hannah had taken great offence. 'How on earth can you be glad not to return?' she'd asked.

Mansoor's parents had been driven out of Lydd by Zionist militias in 1948, escaping to Jordan, where Mansoor had been born.

Mansoor's face had creased as he smiled. 'It was enough to go back in 2000 and see an American Jew living in my parents' home. Seeing that once is enough for a lifetime. I have high blood pressure as it is.'

'Nonsense. Quit the argeela and salty food and visit your house with me. I'll deal with the American.'

Mansoor had snorted.

As for Donya, her family had been driven out of Jaffa in 1948. They fled first to Jordan and then to Lebanon where

Donya had been born, and where two generations of her family remained. For Donya, any disappointment at the change in plans dissolved as soon as she learnt she was to become a grandmother.

'When the baby is a little older,' she'd told Hannah, 'we'll go to Palestine and then Lebanon, visit the family and, if you want, you can get a tummy tuck too.'

'Mum, I'm a feminist,' had been Hannah's response.

'Yes, I know. Which is why I didn't also suggest a boob job. Maybe you'll bottle-feed. Who knows.'

Hannah smiled at the memory as she looked down at Aya. When she was sure that she was fast asleep, she lowered Aya into her cot. She vowed that she would interview her parents before it was too late.

Hannah called her mother as soon as she woke up the next morning. 'It's my day off, Mum,' she said. 'I'm coming over to record your life story. Baba's too.'

'Life story?' Donya let out a laugh. 'Habibti, I'm still living my life.'

'Yes, I know, Mum. But it's important to record this while we can.'

'Are you saying I'm old?'

'No, I'm saying that memory is resistance.'

'You want to sit down with me and I tell you about this and that misery and life in the camps in Lebanon and the civil war and woe is me?' Her mother tsked. 'As you can see, I'm still here laughing and living.'

Hannah took a deep breath. Every conversation with her mother ended up like this.

'But that's exactly why I want to interview you.'

'Habibti, I'm not in the mood,' she said apologetically. 'I'm in the mood for Aya. Bring her here to me and interview your father. He has a better memory anyway.'

Hannah arrived at her parents' doorstep within the hour, armed with a list of questions.

Donya, with blow-dried hair and bright lipstick, squealed when she saw Aya, grabbed her from Hannah and immediately went into besotted-grandmother mode.

'I've made tea and left out ma'moul from Eid,' she called out behind her as she smothered Aya with kisses and ascended the stairs. 'My angel and I will be in my room. I got her a rocking horse.'

'Mum, you already got her a rocking horse.'

'This one plays music,' Donya countered. 'I couldn't resist! Yalla, leave us!'

Hannah and her dad went outside, where they sat under the backyard pergola nursing cups of cinnamon- and cardamom-infused tea. Even at seventy-one, her dad's big hazel eyes sparkled. She placed a notepad, a pile of papers and photographs on the Ikea table between them.

After a few minutes of general family chat, Hannah decided it was time to tell her dad she wanted to interview him.

'About what?'

'Your life.'

'Okay. But you'll need to ask me questions.'

'Okay.'

Hannah looked down at her carefully prepared notes but suddenly felt tongue-tied.

How do you record a life? she thought to herself.

How do you decide what questions matter? How do you repress the panic that you might forget a detail, a piece of family history that will be buried when your father dies and that you'll never be able to find out about? Cut off as you are, from homeland, from family, from the archives of your life looted and destroyed in a stolen village to which you are denied the right of return?

'Start from the beginning,' she said.

'I want a four- or maybe five-part series.' Mansoor fixed his twinkling eyes on her. 'Maybe *60 Minutes*. Actually, *Al Jazeera* so they see it in Lebanon and I become famous. Deal?'

'Yeah, sure, I have the producer in Doha on speed-dial.' She motioned to her phone, opened on the Voice Memos app. 'Yala, Baba. It's recording.'

He contemplated her for some moments, then leant forward and picked up her notepad. He opened it to a blank page and then carefully pulled it out along the perforated edge.

'The beginning? Okay, you see this page?' he asked, holding it up.

She nodded.

'This was us. Don't stare at me confused. I will explain. This page was us across the Middle East, Palestine, Lebanon, Syria, Jordan, Iraq, Arabia.'

He suddenly ripped the paper into pieces. Fragments fell onto the table, and he gathered them into a pile with his callused hands.

'This is colonialism. The British, the French, the Americans. They cut and rip. And then as we try to mend and put together again, they bring a giant fan over us and we are left running to snatch a piece here, a piece there. And sometimes we manage to find some glue, and we stick some pieces together, and they blame us for being so cut up and divided. And they come back, always come back, and they cut and rip us up again …'

Here Mansoor collected some pieces and started ripping them into smaller fragments.

'And, ya, Hannah, they keep the glue from us. They give us tiny bits of it and tell us where we can use it and how much, and always the fan is on, and we are chasing pieces. So, there is *that* beginning. And *my* beginning is on one of those scraps, in a camp in Lebanon.'

A few hours passed as he told her about his life. They drank cups of tea and wolfed down Donya's ma'moul. Hannah's father, an oral encyclopaedia of dates, descriptions, commentary and facts, did not stop talking.

Finally, he fell quiet, depleted from chasing fragments of a diasporic life: Palestine, Jordan, Australia.

Hannah gave her father a hug, accepted a container of lasagna from her mother, uploaded the recording to an online transcription service and went home.

The next morning, Hannah was in the office by 9 am, hunched over her laptop writing an article on a Melbourne teenager who was the lead claimant in a Federal Court class action against the Federal Minister for the Environment. She was transcribing interview responses when her phone rang.

It was Bilal, Nabil's cousin, who she'd exchanged numbers with at the courthouse. She rushed out of the office hub to the quiet corridor leading to the bathrooms.

'Look, Nabil isn't doing too well. He's on remand in Goulburn. Supermax,' Bilal said.

'I'm so sorry, Bilal,' Hannah said.

'Have you seen the stuff about him and the family in the media? They're making him out to be a monster. And the family feels abandoned by the community.'

'What do you mean?'

'People are scared of being linked to us. ASIO's questioning us, putting pressure on his friends, trying to find ways to stitch him up, make it look like he was part of a cell.'

'My God.'

'We need people to know what they're reading about him isn't the truth.'

Hannah, even though she was convinced it would do more harm than good, couldn't bear to say no. She would at least speak to her boss to 'suss him out'.

As it turned out, she had her chance within the hour. John buzzed her desk phone and asked in a suspiciously casual way if she would join him for a chat over coffee at Cult Café at the bottom of their building.

Hannah went to the bathroom for a nervous wee first and then made her way downstairs. It couldn't be about her posts. She'd deleted them. Was it about the open letter that Jeanette had published on the *Do Better* website? Surely not. She was one of hundreds of journalists and members of the Media Entertainment and Arts Alliance who had signed an open letter. It didn't name any outlet, certainly not her employer. She was within her rights.

John was already in the queue, placing his order.

'Can I get you something?' he asked.

She blurted out a 'No, I'm good, thanks', even though she was desperate for a coffee. She'd been raised to always be the one to give, not take, and while it was cultural conditioning that made sense in a big Arab family, it was lost in translation in the corporate world. John didn't press her, and she could have kicked herself for now having to face him for a 'chat' without the fortification of a skim latte.

They engaged in awkward small talk and avoided eye contact as they waited for his coffee order to be called.

John's weekend had been hectic, he told her. Saturday morning family picnic, paint and sip fiftieth birthday party in the evening, gymnastics trials for his daughter on Sunday. He didn't ask her about her weekend. She almost laughed thinking about how she could respond: *Restocked my make-up at MECCA, then spent the next two hours chanting 'Down with the Zionist entity', followed by dinner with friends.*

When they sat down at a quiet corner table, Hannah worked up the courage to tell John that she might have a lead with Nabil's family. She'd avoided doing so until now, worried about the kind of story John would direct her to write.

John was impressed. 'Good work. Dig as much as you can.'

Hannah gave John an account of what Bilal and Samih had revealed, about Nabil's visit to their family's refugee camp in Lebanon and how deeply it had affected him.

'We're not running a soft story, Hannah, if that's what you're proposing. It's not our job to two-sides terrorism.'

'Alleged.'

John waved her comment away and Hannah knew there was no point in pushing back.

'Well,' she ventured instead, 'what about a story about the political process behind proscribing organisations? The influence of interest groups and stakeholders—'

'Absolutely not,' he cut her off. 'And even if we were to run such a story, I'm sorry but you wouldn't be the one to do it.'

Hannah flinched. 'What do you mean?'

'Look, this is actually why I wanted to meet with you.'

Hannah leant back in her chair and braced herself.

'The problem', John explained, carefully, almost warily, 'is that there are several factors that coalesce to cast doubts about your impartiality and neutrality – as a journalist, not as a Palestinian.' He looked pleased that he'd remembered to clarify the point. 'I appreciate how separating the two would be challenging.'

He gave Hannah an almost apologetic smile as he wrapped his thin fingers around his coffee and sat up, pushing the barrel of his designer shirt out.

'The first concern,' he continued, 'is that you filed your Eid story using language that ignored editorial guidelines. You also posted problematic content on social media, although, to your credit' – at this point he offered a nod of approval – 'you deleted the posts. And now you've signed an open letter that could be perceived as pushing an agenda. That could open you to criticism that you are being an activist for a cause.'

Hannah understood then that this would not be a meeting of open censure, clear directives or explicit commands. She was to be handled with the language liberals love best: equivocation and obfuscation. It would be death by a thousand white-liberal cuts.

John grimaced and she interpreted this as his way of attempting to assuage her that he felt conflicted, burdened.

It was a classic shoot-and-cry move. If only he knew the depth of her contempt.

'I can't ask you to withdraw your name', he mused, 'and by no means am I suggesting that you'll be subjected to any retribution for aligning yourself with the letter. But it's in your *best interests*' – and here, he paused, for effect – 'that you not take sides, that you reconsider.'

Hannah paused too, drew breath as her mind whirred, trying to formulate her own arguments, winding up for a return serve.

Would she recite the names of colleagues who had enjoyed accolades and awards for their 'brave', 'courageous', 'uncompromising' articles, reports and books on child sexual abuse in the church, domestic violence, same-sex marriage?

She wanted to ask him: *Have you heard of Santiago Castro-Gómez's 'point zero perspective'? No? Well, let me enlighten you, John! The point zero perspective is the Western myth of a point of view that assumes itself to be beyond a point of view. Confronted with genocide, ethnic cleansing, occupation and apartheid, claiming that you are not taking sides* is *taking sides, John.*

But John was no fool. He had convened the meeting fully prepared for Hannah's rebuttals and had mapped out his pre-emptive strikes. She didn't stand a chance. He forged ahead before she even had a chance to utter Castro-Gómez's name.

'I want to assure you that nobody is forcing you to do anything. If your name remains on the open letter it will impact the stories you can cover, but nobody, I repeat, *nobody* here is compelling you to withdraw. We respect your right to sign the statement.'

He said he'd give her time to think about it and excused himself, saying he had another meeting.

After dinner, Jamal showed her the message he'd received from his sister that morning. Hannah started reading:

> Things are messed up in Gaza and I don't know what to do. It's hard to comprehend what's going on. Our close neighbour has just received a warning phone call to leave his house in preparation for Israeli warplanes to bomb it. Their house is located, as is ours, in an extremely crowded area. If this warning is accurate we anticipate that a drone will fire a warning giving us 5 to 10 minutes to leave the premises, assuming that there is a warning. Should we all go down to the first floor? Or simply stay where we are on the second floor? Anyway no safe place, yallah. We will see what Allah has written for us, if we survive we will, and if not, then to a better life for sure than this hell.

Hannah looked up at Jamal with concern as she handed back his phone.

'If you keep your signature,' he said gently, 'then you're signing away your ability to write about this in the mainstream.' He waved his phone. 'If you remove your signature, you're signing up to write about it.'

'It's unfair,' Hannah said. 'That's not a choice.'

'No,' Jamal said bitterly. 'You're right and wrong, no matter which you choose.'

Hannah did what she often did when she felt overwhelmed: she had a good cry in a hot shower.

When she got out, she texted Jeanette: *Pls remove my name.*

Jeanette responded instantly: *Are you okay? MEAA's releasing a statement tomorrow defending journalists' right to sign.*

Hannah texted back: *Not okay. But I'll be fine. Send me your trashiest, brain-cell killing series recs. I need some escapism.*

25

Ashraf walked into the school foyer and approached the front desk. The receptionist motioned at him to sign in and to take a seat. He waited on a grey Ikea-looking armchair outside Fayza's office.

The door swung open, and a young teacher stepped out, puffy-eyed and with tissues scrunched in her hand. Fayza emerged with her and gave her a reassuring nod.

Fayza's eyes fell on Ashraf. She smiled and invited him into her office.

'So, what brings you here?' Fayza asked as she sat behind her desk, gesturing for Ashraf to sit in the chair opposite. 'Your message was rather cryptic. "Irresistible and exciting prospect for your students."'

Ashraf was about to respond but was interrupted by a female staff member popping her head in, urgently needing Fayza's signature ('So we can place the sausage order for the athletics carnival') – immediately followed by another teacher bursting in to ask Fayza to authorise admin to send a note out to parents on the portal saying the afternoon's

Year 5 excursion to the Powerhouse Museum had to be cancelled (because she had forgotten to book the bus).

Fayza finally turned to Ashraf again but was cut off by yet another teacher, who appeared in the doorway for just a moment to give Fayza two thumbs up.

'Thank God that's over,' Fayza said.

Ashraf gave her a quizzical look.

'We've had a bit of an investigation going on at school.'

Curiosity aroused and his imagination chasing scenarios of another Nabil, Ashraf sat up straighter. 'Oh? Everything okay?'

'Year 8 girls caught on camera handing vapes to other Year 8 girls. It wasn't clear from the angle whether the currency was money or make-up. But between me and Ms Fadl, who you just saw, we got a confession.'

'Oh!' Ashraf smiled. 'Vaping. Is that the way to get suspended these days?'

'One of them,' Fayza said. 'But in this case, it was a one-off, and hardly a sophisticated black-market enterprise. That's the Year 10 students. Entrepreneurial skills that would put high-flying corporate execs to shame.'

Fayza's computer pinged with a notification. She turned to her screen and frowned in concentration.

'Sorry, Ashraf. As you can see there's never a dull moment here. I have a pile of emails to respond to before introducing a Year 11 incursion in an hour. You said you wanted to talk? You have a proposal?'

Ashraf trod cautiously, mustering a tone of enthusiasm and authority. He explained that he had a fully funded opportunity to get kids involved in a creative project, a project he would personally be overseeing and that she could therefore trust.

Fayza was, to his relief, enthusiastic.

'We have some extremely talented artistic students in the senior years,' she enthused. 'They're highly engaged and motivated. The range of personal interest topics has been incredible. Climate change, consumer fashion, AI, sports, social media and advertising. I can think of at least twenty who would be very keen to do this. Would you run it here? Or at JBU?'

Ashraf couldn't contain his delight.

'Whatever you consider more appropriate and convenient. It really is a collaborative project and your input is just as valuable in shaping our approach and outcomes. I have funding to set up a website and publish the zines there – with full attribution to the students and school, of course. And I'll be writing a report at the end of the project, discussing the aims, process and outcomes, and of course student anonymity will be maintained in any quotes or reflections I write.'

'That's no problem,' Fayza said. As an afterthought, she suddenly asked: 'After all the controversy at JBU, and Nabil's connection to us here, do you think they'll have an issue funding a project for our students?' She laughed and shook her head. 'Universities really are masterful at speaking out of two sides of their mouths.'

Ashraf shifted in his seat. 'Well, the project isn't funded by JBU …' He trailed off.

'Oh, have you left them?'

'No, no, I'm still there.' He let out a hollow laugh. 'I'm still there.'

She waited for him to explain.

'So, this project is government funded. I was approached, headhunted one might say, to do this. It's an excellent opportunity. Our community is always so starved for funding to run good, solid, constructive programs.'

A flush of concern passed over Fayza's face. She pursed her lips and fixed Ashraf with a discerning look. 'What kind of government funding? Which department and program?'

Ashraf knew the collaboration would go no further. It was over before it even started. He was sick of everyone's moral purity.

He said, matter-of-factly, unapologetically, 'Department of Home Affairs.'

'Those grants are counter-radicalisation work by another name,' she said.

'This is your chance to redeem your school's reputation. How do you expect to counter the media campaign against you and your students? By sticking your head in the sand?'

Fayza erupted in anger. 'I've had ASIO here, at my school, interviewing my students, Ashraf. My own daughter!

Simply because they were in the same class as Nabil. I can't believe you would come to me with this,' she said. 'I won't take a cent of that money. I'm not legitimising my students being treated as problems the government needs to solve.'

'It's your tax money too,' he pushed. 'Why shouldn't we use it if it's being offered *for* our community?' He was on his feet now. There was no point lingering.

Fayza stood up too, resting her fingers on her desk.

'Mya was right about you,' she said, her eyes narrowing. 'You don't stand for anything.'

There was nothing left to be said. He was surrounded by self-righteous fools.

He stormed out.

26

Hannah was sitting on a very uncomfortable chair in a crowded bookshop. She had been dragged along by Jamal to a book launch for his department's research director, Leigh Carter, to provide him with moral support.

Jamal had reasoned that, after Jessica Heaton's hit piece (which had been picked up by *Sky News Daily* and turned into the focus of a segment on extremism in education featuring the Shadow Education Minister Fiona Jackson: 'What we need, Sharon, is more stringent student visa vetting mechanisms so that scholarships are awarded to the right kind of people'), it would be wise to keep Leigh on side. Attending her book launch was one way to do this.

He'd told Hannah that he didn't have any other choice. If there were veiled threats to his scholarship and teaching, if he was to be cast as a liability, he needed an ally in management, even if he couldn't quite figure her out.

With a manager like Barnaby, Jamal had said on the drive over, he knew where he stood. To Barnaby, the dean of political science, Jamal wasn't an academic but a

KPI in a budget spreadsheet. Leigh, on the other hand, actually seemed to believe in something but had, like most privileged academics Jamal had encountered, never really been put to the test – and nothing tested progressives more than Palestine.

Barnaby, who was introducing Leigh, clearly held her in high esteem. His tone was one of genuine warmth as he listed her many accolades and introduced her new book *The Sexual Politics of the Haitian War of Independence, 1802–1804*, which he described as 'a fascinating exploration of the question of whether gender was as operative a concept as race, citizenship or class in Saint-Domingue'.

Leigh was, Barnaby gushed, one of Australia's leading authorities on African American slave revolts. Her first book, *From the Stono Rebellion to the German Coast Uprising: Seven decades of resistance*, had won what seemed like a zillion history prizes. *Enslaved African People: Slavery and resistance as restless bedfellows* won another zillion and landed her a prestigious Future Fellowship. She had just finished serving her second term as President of the Australian and New Zealand American Studies Collective.

Hannah watched as Leigh sat on a stool beside Barnaby, a modest smile planted on her face. She was a tall woman, and her long legs in navy slacks dangled from the stool, her red ballet flats (matching her red lipstick, the only make-up on her otherwise bare face) touching the floor. Her hair was long, thick and brown with grey strands running through.

It was a long introduction. Out of the corner of her eye, Hannah could see Jamal's carefully constructed polite façade as he watched Barnaby.

Bored, Hannah started scrolling through her phone. There was a message from Bilal, Nabil's cousin, asking her if she'd heard from her boss. She'd been putting off telling him. She'd just felt too guilty.

Sorry, Bilal, she wrote. *He's not interested in the kind of story you want to tell.*

Bilal responded with an angry emoji and simply: *thanks for trying.*

Finally, Barnaby kicked off the in-conversation. Before responding to his first question – 'With respect to a planter's domination of his female slaves in colonial times, and of his male slaves' powerlessness, to what extent did sex represent power?' – and despite the launch convenor's acknowledgement at the opening of the event, Leigh insisted on first offering her own solemn acknowledgment of country.

Hannah had been reluctant to attend Leigh's book launch because she felt as though she was crashing a clique, rocking up to a Halloween party dressed for Christmas. She didn't begrudge academics their obtuse, verbose jargon. Every profession had its own inner circles and internal codes. What she had no patience for was people who built careers on interpreting the world but who had no desire to change it. Jamal joked that for somebody who didn't have much time for humanities academics, she was a surprisingly good Marxist.

It did grieve her, this wasted industry of diagnosis and abstract cure. It was the state of the world that interested Hannah. She was born with an irrepressible, some (like her cousin Yasmin, who just wanted to enjoy her Shein packages in peace) might say insufferable, passion for fairness, for justice.

When, at last, the formal part of the evening was over, Hannah took refuge at the refreshments table. The book-signing line, predominantly Anglo faces, snaked down the narrow stairs. She sipped mineral water and waited for Jamal, avoiding eye contact with other attendees by keeping her head in her phone.

An account she didn't recognise had tagged her in an Instagram post that was just screenshot after screenshot of her article about Liliana's family with the caption: 'I don't know who needs to hear this, but if you're a journalist of colour in mainstream media and you're using diluted language, you're really just a stenographer perpetuating the pro-Israel status quo and defanging our movement.'

There were twenty-two comments underneath. They came from all directions, some in support of the poster, some sympathetic to Hannah: 'Real estate dispute? Scuffles? These are gross euphemisms! Shame!'; 'Thank you, Hannah, for giving a voice to a Palestinian family'; 'Why is this article calling Hamas wholesale a terrorist organisation? Fact check: only the paramilitary wing of Hamas is designated'; 'babes, you'll never reform a broken system, master's tools and all'; 'This article is heart-breaking. I can't believe *The Chronicle* actually published it. Don't let perfect be the enemy of the good'; 'You're not even Palestinian and you're dragging a Palestinian woman? WTF?!'

From the supportive to the oppositional, every response was, she had to admit, legitimate. Hannah had been a journalist for some time now. She was no stranger to the comments section – to death and rape threats in her DMs, interspersed with messages of support and praise. She didn't feel surprised, upset or validated. She just felt gross.

Hannah opened her email and was pleased to see that the word file transcribing her interview with her father had been sent. Jamal was still waiting in the queue for his book to be signed, so she sat back down and started reading.

Speaker 1: Okay, Dad, we're going to start right from the beginning. Can you tell me your mum and dad's full names?

Speaker 2: My mother's name [inaudible]. My father Mahmud [inaudible].

Speaker 1: And your grandparents?

Speaker 2: [Inaudible]

Speaker 1: What were your siblings' names?

Speaker 2: I had five. [Inaudible]

Speaker 1: And what camp were you born in?

Speaker 2: [Inaudible]

Hannah was a journalist. She couldn't help herself. She saw metaphors everywhere.

Hannah and Jamal had spent the morning furiously cleaning the apartment in advance of a house inspection at noon. Their landlord had been sending tradies to fix various issues, leading Hannah to suspect that the owner was gearing up to sell, but Jamal, who preferred to triage his stress in order of actual problems, not speculation, brushed off her worries and suggested they simply get the house tidied up and spend the day fishing and picnicking as a family at Church Point.

'I feel suffocated,' he'd said. 'I need a recharge. We both do.'

And so here they were on the beach at Church Point on this warm and bright day. A few people waded out into the shallows with rods and nets. Dinghies and pedal boats dotted the water.

Jamal cast his line into the channel while Hannah, with Aya balanced on her hip so she couldn't crawl away, set up the picnic blanket and food. The three of them were just settling down to eat and relax when Hannah's phone started ringing.

She almost missed the call. It wasn't a number she recognised and she was slow to pick up because Aya was fussing over her pureed pumpkin. Jamal had copped a bright-orange blob of it on his t-shirt and was frantically trying to clean it off.

The voice at the end of the line was unfamiliar to her. A little haughty, a little no-nonsense.

'Sorry, who's this?' Hannah asked.

'It's Fayza Sayid, Principal of Al-Bayinnah Islamic College.'

Hannah practically threw Aya into Jamal's arms, smudging the pumpkin stain even more. He protested, but she ignored him and moved away from the picnic blanket, trying to find somewhere quiet.

She couldn't believe it: Fayza wanted to meet her. To be interviewed. To tell her side of the story.

The school had received death threats, abusive emails and graffiti. Yesterday, two students were accosted by a reporter from *The Daily Letter* wanting information about Nabil and 'other extremist students at the school'. It was time to set the record straight, to hit back at the racist smear campaign.

As soon as she finished the call, Hannah emailed John as she walked back to Jamal and Aya.

John responded within moments. He congratulated Hannah for landing the story, for cultivating enough trust with the principal that she had approached her. He then instructed Hannah to co-write the story with Peter and also have him attend the interview.

'Fuck!'

Jamal looked at Hannah with concern.

She gave him an account of her conversation with Fayza and John's directive.

'Is this because you don't trust me to do justice to the story?' she typed, saying the words aloud for Jamal's benefit.

Seconds later, Hannah read out John's response: 'The piece will be stronger with more than one byline.'

While Jamal snuggled Aya in his arms, cleaned her face and hands with a wet wipe and gave her some water, Hannah bashed out another email, reading aloud: 'But Peter's already written an article and, given its angle, I don't think the principal's going to be as forthcoming when we meet if he's there too.'

'Yes, it's weird he'd assume Fayza would agree to proceed,' Jamal said.

Hannah closed her eyes. 'My head hurts.'

'Put the phone away and just switch off,' he said gently, handing her a bottle of water.

But, as he spoke, her phone buzzed again. And again.

It was the media WhatsApp group chat. Danny had sent a photo of *The Australian Times*' front page that day. A photo of a Palestinian teenager throwing a stone, headline: *Fighting Spreads to West Bank: Three people die in clashes.*

Rima was furious: *Clashes! And who are the people who died, huh?*

Hannah sent three angry emojis to the chat.

'Enough messages, Hannah,' Jamal pleaded.

Not looking up, she reassured him it was her last message.

Her phone pinged again.

'It's John!' she cried, opening the email. '"Peter's article was written the way it was precisely because the principal shut you out. He had no other options. Now she has an opportunity for people to hear *her* side of the story and for your intervention with this new piece to cut through the reporting we've seen from the tabloids. I think it's an excellent opportunity for you." Why does he always turn it around so it looks like I'm the unreasonable one?'

'Can we just leave this all for an hour?' Jamal said, exasperated. 'John will be there gaslighting you when we get to the car. And Peter will be there patronising you on our drive home, which is when we can talk it through. But we agreed to come here for a small timeout, Hannah. Just take a moment to hotspot some of this good energy out here.'

'Yes, yes, I know,' Hannah said with regret.

She took Aya from Jamal and cuddled her close, but then her phone started to ring. She looked down at the screen.

It was only-calls-if-urgent-Jeanette. Hannah gave Jamal a rueful look.

He stood up abruptly and walked to the water to check on his fishing line.

Feeling guilty, but also feeling she had no choice – what was even the point of indulging the delusion that they could pursue normality in such times? – Hannah took the call and spent the next half hour consoling Jeanette, who had just ended things with her boyfriend because he couldn't handle how traumatised she was by what was happening in Gaza. She loved him, but they were too broke for couples therapy and she was too committed to look away.

27

Ashraf knew he needed to find a way to deal with Jamal and that he couldn't put it off any longer. He invited Jamal to meet for a coffee in the central courtyard at lunchtime.

He listened to Jamal vent, offering words of sympathy and understanding about the article ('Sensationalised trash. It was bordering on defamation, but who has the money to sue corporate media? That's why they get away with it! I'm so sorry you're going through this, Jamal'), and about the solidarity statement and whether it had a good response ('Hundreds of signatures? That's so impressive. A vindication of your dogged pursuit of justice, Jamal').

Jamal also spoke about his family. He and his wife were barely sleeping these days, up all night watching the news or exchanging WhatsApp messages with Jamal's family.

'God protect them,' Ashraf said. 'Any chance they can get out? Once there's a ceasefire, inshAllah?'

'They hit my uncle's home last week,' Jamal said, twisting a napkin in his hand. 'It's gone, completely destroyed. He insists on sleeping on top of the rubble. He refuses to leave. Once there's a ceasefire, he'll rebuild it as many times as they bomb it. But he'll never leave.'

While Jamal spoke, Ashraf nodded along, waiting for a suitable break in the conversation.

'I'm sorry to burden you with my own stress at this time, Jamal,' Ashraf said. 'God knows you have enough on your plate.'

Jamal appeared affronted. '*Burden*? You've been my main support. How can you say that?'

'Thank you, Jamal,' he said, with a sheepish half-smile. 'You're probably too consumed with Gaza – rightly so – to have noticed the staff cuts and forced redundancies. University of Western Sydney laid off staff last week. University of Technology Sydney announced massive redundancies too.'

'Of course I've noticed,' Jamal said. 'Gaza doesn't mean we get to hit pause on the crises and problems here. If only life was so merciful … It's all connected anyway.'

'There are talks about cuts here, at JBU, which puts me' – and here he sighed with dramatic effect – 'into a bind.'

Jamal leant forward, listening with concern.

'Management will go after the lowest hanging fruit,' Ashraf explained. 'This new project pushed me up a few branches. I think I might just be safe – for now. But there's possibly nothing more likely to push me down again than political controversy over Palestine.'

Jamal looked puzzled. 'But what controversy? You haven't signed anything. Have you made any public statements?

Were you at the rally? Surely that's okay anyway? It's not as though you gave a speech. Were you there?'

Ashraf nodded. It was a white lie. He had met up with a friend for lunch in the city and heard the protesters as they marched past the building. He had, one might argue, technically been there.

'Oh, I didn't see you. Did you hear my speech?'

'No, I'm sorry. I was late and missed the speeches.'

Jamal smiled. 'Well, thanks to Jessica Heaton, you got a chance to read it.'

'The difficulty for me, the injustice of this all, is that the controversy attached to you will, by virtue of your proximity to me, attach to me ...'

Jamal looked mortified. 'I'm so sorry.'

'No, no,' Ashraf quickly countered. 'This is not your fault.'

'What a terrible situation,' Jamal said. 'Is there anything I can do? We need you in the academy. Most of the people in Middle East studies aren't even Middle Eastern. We can't afford to lose you.'

Ashraf leant back in his chair, exhaled and crossed his legs under the table. 'It's insidious,' he said. 'What we need to do is operate more strategically, play the long game, have a vision. What I want is to build Arab representation in this field. I want to see you, Jamal, pursue an academic career, build up the next generation.'

'InshAllah.'

Ashraf rubbed the back of his neck. He was exhausted. The academy was like one big chess board. His head hurt thinking about all the moves he had to make, all the plays he had to set up, knowing that he would never have the power of checkmate, not in a game that was rigged against him from the start. He had to turn on his own, sacrifice his pieces, to protect himself, to move slightly ahead.

He took a deep breath. 'I hope you understand that I'll need you to step back a little, from me.'

'I understand,' Jamal said, looking downcast. 'What do you need from me?'

'I'm so sorry to ask, it seems so trivial, if you could delete my name from your email signature?'

'Okay, sure.'

'And I'll need to take you off my Youth Power project.'

'Oh. Okay.' Jamal seemed surprised.

'What a bind.' Ashraf swallowed hard. 'All such projects have strings attached, obviously, but really it's not strings they've attached – it's rope.'

'I understand,' Jamal reassured him. 'I would never want to be the cause of somebody, especially somebody in your position, losing their job. Not just because you've been good to me. But because your job is linked to so many opportunities for others too.'

'Thank you, Jamal,' he said. 'I'll remain your supervisor. I've looked into things and there's nobody else with capacity to take over.'

'Oh? I didn't even think about that.' Jamal stared at the floor. 'Wow. That bad, huh?'

'I'm so sorry, Jamal.'

'No, it's okay. So, what do I tell the group that was going to be in the project?'

'Well, it was never guaranteed. We're still going through ethics. Just tell them things fell through.'

'And do you have an alternative?'

'I'm working on it.'

They sat in silence for a few moments. Jamal played with a sugar packet, tapping it against his cup. Ashraf stared out at the crowded, bustling courtyard, filled with students.

Finally, Ashraf spoke: 'It really, really pains me to ask all this of you, Jamal.'

And it did. It was excruciating, in fact. He'd tried to explain that he felt like he was stuck in a tiny corner in a large structure and that, because it was impossible to tear the whole thing down, he would at least try to make his small corner as strong and as special a space as he could.

Maybe, by doing so, it would draw more people to his corner and slowly they'd build the corner into a room and that room into two rooms and eventually they would take up a larger space in the structure and be able to renovate and then, finally, knock down and rebuild.

Did Jamal understand this was not personal? Did he understand the big, sorry picture? That they were, and this was so crucial, *all* victims here?

28

Hannah was on her way to Al-Bayinnah, skolling a Red Bull as she sat in midmorning traffic on the Hume Highway.

She'd hoped to leave home early, but she and Jamal had gone to bed late, watching the news and messaging back and forth with Jamal's family. They ended up sleeping through fajr prayer and the alarm.

Hannah turned up the volume on the ABC news. US Secretary of State Antony Blinken was going on about the US having a 'commitment to giving Israel the means to defend itself'. Meanwhile, Palestinian officials were estimating reconstruction costs in the tens of millions of dollars.

Hannah needed to settle her heart. She couldn't keep up with this frenzied pace. She Hey-Siri'd Spotify to play the Quran and relaxed her hands on the steering wheel as she moved along at 15 miles an hour, although it was difficult to feel any sense of peace as a Mercedes C63 in the next lane blasted Nicki Minaj (and not a clean version) with the windows down.

Peter had suggested they meet at the office and carpool to Al-Bayinnah, but Hannah, whose skin crawled at the thought of such proximity, lied and said she had an errand to run after the school meeting before heading into the office and so preferred to drive separately. Peter had sounded disappointed, saying he'd hoped, given he lived in Coogee and almost never ventured so far out west, that they could grab a bite from 'the famous Jasmin 1', seven minutes from the school according to Google Maps, on their way back to the office. 'Feel free to go by yourself. I'm not into Jasmine 1,' was her imperious rebuff.

Later, as she thought about their conversation while scrolling through the latest headlines – *Israeli Air Raids Pounding Gaza* – Hannah turned over her response in her mind. Had she been rude and unfair to Peter?

Was this an example of what Jamal's academic friend Jude called racial hypochondria, of seeing race in everything when Peter, put aside how much she detested him, could simply have been craving a mixed plate and fatta? Or had she earnt the right to be perennially suspicious and irritated by White people with a capital *W*? And, if she had, was she – and she considered this question as she watched a video of settler lynch mobs rampaging through Nablus – losing her capacity to triage her anger? But wasn't it all connected? *Feck!* (Her new word. She was trying *so* hard.) She felt like there was a constant game of Tetris being played inside her head, blocks of thought descending slowly at first and then faster and faster until she could no longer put them in order.

Hannah and Peter drove into the car park at Al-Bayinnah at almost the same time. There was ample visitor parking. Hannah pulled into a spot, grabbed her bag and exited the car. She had taken special care to dress up today: a black power suit, high heels and hair slicked back into a bun in an effort to project confidence and authority despite the demeaning effect of Peter's presence.

She glanced over at Peter, who'd parked further away and was checking his appearance in the rear-view mirror. She waited for him. He soon emerged and walked towards her, a small black leather notebook in his hand. He was utterly oblivious to her sense of injury at his role of white alibi.

First offering an inscrutable smile, Hannah took the lead to the front office. She focused on trying to slow down the rapidly descending Tetris blocks. If she failed to self-regulate, she'd mess up and it would be over before it started. John would be vindicated in insisting on Peter's presence after all, even though the cause of her emotional spiral was precisely his presence.

My God, white supremacy is fecking genius.

They had arrived mid-recess and the school grounds were swarming with noisy students and teachers on duty.

Hannah watched Peter as he gazed around, soaking it all in, slowing down to take notes as he walked. He stopped to take a photo on his phone of the Tupac mural. She tried to imagine how Peter was coding the sights around him: the hijabs on girls; the huge cultural mix of teachers on duty, including a few Anglo teachers; the murals and posters foregrounding Islam.

Hannah had done a few stories at various schools across Sydney before and always felt a little nervous walking into a school. It was its own ecosystem and there was something both charming and utterly terrifying about making one's way as an adult through a playground filled with a mix of noisy, wild, friendly, sullen, joyful, boisterous students looking you up and down, sensing your outside status.

As she walked beside Peter, though, she felt less like an outsider. She didn't know a single person at the school, but she felt bound to them and that stirred something fiercely protective in her. She was ready to pounce if he dared say something judgemental, sarcastic or plain stupid, but he seemed, what an irony, neutral.

Fayza was standing at the door to the front office, waiting. She smiled as they approached and welcomed them inside.

After John had emailed Hannah, she'd immediately called Fayza and checked if it was okay for Peter to join as co-author of the article given the pieces he'd written so far. Fayza's response, 'I trust him if you do,' had pierced her. She'd avoided a direct answer, opting instead to reassure Fayza that, given Hannah's byline would be on the article too, she would fight to ensure that it countered the hysterical sensationalist reporting so far. She was determined to wield every last part of her cultural and religious authority against Peter and John to insist on the final shape and tone of the published article. And she promised as much to Fayza.

Peter invited Hannah to ask questions of Fayza first, a gesture Hannah appreciated. She'd been nervous that he would assume the lead.

Hannah focused on the burdens placed on teachers and schools. What do you say to people who blame teachers for not picking up those students on a path to radicalisation? Do you think this is an unfair expectation on teachers and misunderstands the role of teachers? And how do you even navigate this when radicalisation is so politicised?

Fayza sat up, her face animated.

'There's a sense of déjà vu for those of us who were teaching during the hysteria over some teenagers running off to join ISIS a few years back. You probably don't remember. My particular favourite was the nervous breakdown over some senior kids at Surryville Boys' who wouldn't shake hands with female teachers at an award ceremony, but instead,' said Fayza, demonstrating the action, 'placing their hands across their chest as a mark of respect like this.' It was all over the news, even got picked up by Fox and *The Independent.* They were all losing their minds.'

'Yes, I remember that,' Peter said. 'It was a daily media barrage linking ISIS and Muslim youth.'

'Precisely,' Fayza said.

'I mean, there were some cases of teenagers running off to join ISIS.'

Fayza nodded. 'Yes, there were. But the media and political debate at the time—'

'It was all generalisations about an entire community.'

'Yes, exactly,' Fayza said with an air of surprise.

Hannah was just as struck by Peter's reasonable responses.

'Fast forward a few years,' Fayza continued. 'There's been the Christchurch terrorist attack – but always describe him as a lone wolf. Throw in the rise of Trump and mainstreaming of the far right – but don't admit that you empowered them. There's a new generation, like Nabil, who sees our government selling weapons to Israel to drop bombs on Palestinians, sees our government having no issue with Australians serving in the IDF, killing Palestinians one year and coming back to their lives in Australia the next, sees the cheapness of Muslim blood. Naively, Nabil engages in an act of protest not understanding the legal implications.'

'Surely he knows Hamas is a terror organisation?' Peter interjected.

'Hamas is defined as a terror organisation by a government allied to Israel,' Hannah said in a flat tone.

'Exactly. A *terror* organisation,' Peter said.

'Do you know,' Fayza said, 'we teach a Year 11 subject on theories of knowledge. We start with a famous exchange between Humpty Dumpty and Alice.'

Hannah raised an eyebrow.

'It's true,' Fayza said. 'Humpty Dumpty says to Alice, "When *I* use a word it means just what I choose it to mean – neither more nor less." And Alice says, "The question is, whether you *can* make a word mean so many different things." And Humpty Dumpty replies, "The question is, which is to be master – that's all."'

'I'm sorry, but terrorism isn't relative,' Peter said.

Hannah laughed.

'You think this is funny?' Peter said.

'My people are, as we speak, being bombed, Peter,' Hannah said.

Fayza flicked her gaze between Peter and Hannah and said, 'Let me finish. I'm not pro-Hamas, by the way. I'm a pacifist.'

Hannah watched Peter – there was no mistaking his relief.

'I believe that diplomacy and international law,' she continued, 'are the only way forward for Palestinians.'

Yeah, how's that working out for them? Hannah thought to herself.

'We teach our students to respect the law.' Fayza hesitated.

Hannah recognised the look on Fayza's face. It was an expression that was familiar to her: the anxiety of speaking in a minefield, dodging words loaded with dangerous matter, combustible meanings.

Fayza continued, 'I mentioned the Humpty Dumpty lesson because, and it pains me to say this, while we teach our students that they should feel a sense of belonging to this nation as Australian Muslims, we need them to be aware that the laws of this place actually work against them. When laws can mean different things for different people, there's a greater need for us to teach our youth to be vigilant about what they say and do. We want our students to feel a strong sense of identity as Australian Muslims and to also understand how to navigate the challenges of belonging.'

Fayza's response didn't sit well with Hannah. What had trying to belong to a settler colony ever achieved for them? Not safety. Weren't they just setting up young Muslims for failure? Couldn't they embrace a different vision? Recognise whose stolen land they were on and where their loyalties should lie? She longed to invite Fayza to reflect on these questions, not in the spirit of accusation but as a way of working through what she sensed were agonising external pressures and expectations.

But there was no way she could push back with Peter in the room. She feared she'd already done enough damage and walked Fayza into a discussion that it would have been better to avoid. What on earth would Peter take from all of this? Why couldn't she have kept her stupid mouth shut and let him have his terrorism rant?

Peter asked if they could interview some students.

Fayza politely declined. 'There's been enough focus on them and I won't have my students exposed anymore.'

Instead, Fayza invited them to take a short tour of the school and, turning to Peter, suggested that he could pose his interview questions as they walked.

He took up the idea with enthusiasm.

To Hannah's complete surprise – a sentiment that Fayza likely shared, given her keen engagement – Peter proceeded to ask all the right questions: How have students and staff been impacted by the Islamophobic backlash on Islamic schooling? There are suggestions, albeit by a minority of parents, that you prioritise religion over secular education, but is that a fair criticism given this is an Islamic school and religion would obviously play a large role in students' overall education? Do the students feel Al-Bayinnah is a safe space for them?

Hannah was confused by Peter's apparent engagement.

As they walked through the school grounds, Peter was particularly fascinated by the clear prominence of Palestinian-themed artworks, posters, banners and stickers around the school. He sought permission to take photos and Fayza nodded her approval.

'Is there a sizeable Palestinian student cohort at the school?' he asked.

'No,' Fayza said. 'We do have some families. The cousin and aunt of one student were killed on the third day of the bombing.'

'That's terrible,' Peter said. 'So many innocent lives caught up in the violence.'

‘Caught up? Or killed?’ Hannah blurted out.

Peter glanced at Hannah but didn’t respond.

‘How have students in Nabil’s class been affected?’ Hannah asked. ‘He was arrested for protesting a university’s weapons contracts with Israel. And, in the background of his arrest, Gaza is being bombed. How are they even processing this?’

‘They’re outraged, worried sick for Nabil. We’ve had a few guest speakers to help the students process it all, not just what happened to Nabil but also what’s happening in Gaza. From a religious perspective, a mental health perspective. It’s a strong focus in the Friday sermons.’

Having brought them almost all the way back to the office, Fayza stopped outside the art room. It was empty of students, and she invited them to take a look inside.

Peter did a slow lap around the artworks and installations, pausing to study the paintings and sculptures.

‘Everybody here’s deeply affected by what’s happening,’ Fayza said. ‘Palestine’s clearly not an exclusively Muslim cause, but for Muslims it’s a core Islamic struggle.’

Peter murmured, ‘It’s evidently a unifying part of your school’s culture.’

‘Ramadan’s been different this year. We’ve come together as a school in solidarity – the students are driving it, in fact – running fundraisers, cupcake stalls, poetry events, and art and writing competitions.’

‘But for Nabil that wasn’t enough,’ Peter said casually. ‘It seems the school offers a safe space for students to express their solidarity. But for Nabil, and he's only one of … How many students did you say there are here?'

'Around six hundred.'

'One in six hundred who took that extreme step. I mean, it's hardly a radicalisation incubator here as has been reported.'

Fayza gave him an inscrutable look. 'Yes, exactly,' she said.

'I guess it also depends on who defines extreme,' Hannah added.

Peter stopped in front of the two decorated mannequins – thobe man and Barbie hijabi keffiyeh girl – and began taking photographs from various angles.

'This was a final year art project last year,' Fayza explained. 'Shireen Tofaha. One of our brightest students.'

On their way out, Fayza asked Peter and Hannah to clarify the story angle. She reiterated that she had 'agreed to an interview to offer a fair insight into the impact of Nabil's arrest, and the media and political backlash' on her students, and to also 'demystify Islamic schooling' and 'counter the misinformation and stereotypes'.

Hannah, backed by Peter, reassured her they would do the school justice.

29

Ashraf was chopping up salad ingredients for his dinner, feeling elated. He'd received an email on his way home from work informing him that his paper 'Lessons from tribal solidarity' had been accepted in one of the top-ranking journals in his field. He'd submitted it over a year earlier and it had taken almost thirteen months for the journal to referee it and reach a decision.

His paper explored the concept of al fazaa'a, meaning a surge of solidarity offered by tribes called upon for help in war, and reflected on whether it could be used as a theoretical comparative framework for understanding the Arab Spring in Tunisia and the Occupy Wall Street movement. How, Ashraf had asked, can activists use their strength in numbers to shift the balance of power?

To be accepted by this journal was as esteemed a commendation as one could hope for. He emailed Leigh (who was thrilled for him) and Brendan (*Mabruk!* he replied), and, with nobody else to share the news with, sent his daughters a message.

They messaged back: *Congratulations, Dad!*

He would take it.

He sat down to eat and began catching up with the news. Talks of a ceasefire, thank God. The protests would stop, this heightened state of crisis could dissipate and things would calm down.

His phone rang and Simon's name came up on the screen. He grabbed his phone and, with apprehension, answered.

Simon was calling with some 'concerns'. Ashraf's heart sank. He was 'checking in' as he noticed the ethics application and project proposal had been amended. Having done some 'due diligence', he could well understand why Ash had taken Jamal off the project, but he just wanted to 'be certain' that there would be no further 'issues'.

Ashraf was quick to reassure Simon that Jamal had been taken care of and that the project was safe. He told him how, just yesterday, he'd had confirmation from a mosque he'd reached out to in Granville that a group of young Muslim men from a community group there were lined up for the initiative.

'They're *very* keen as they missed out on the last round of grants and rely on community donations for all their initiatives. All volunteers. This will be a game changer for them. There's a group of about thirty-five young people, nineteen to twenty-two years old.'

Simon was satisfied.

Crisis averted.

30

Hannah felt Jamal rousing her for fajr prayer. He gently shook her, then planted a kiss on her shoulder.

'Come on,' he whispered.

She forced herself to rise and perform her ablution, and then joined him for prayer.

It was in these moments that Hannah felt the most grateful and blessed to have Jamal as her naseeb. Their shared spirituality meant they were navigating the same roadmap in their marriage. She loved so much about him independent of the love she had for him as the father of her child. That could never be enough for her.

She loved Jamal in his own right. His patience (she'd seen him go through five failed password attempts in a row without so much as cracking a frown), his kindness (it was his habit to always call her on his way home to check if she needed anything), his hygiene (he was a minimum two-showers-a-day person), his integrity, his attentiveness to her parents, his irrepressible imagination, but above all Hannah loved Jamal's unwavering God-consciousness. It meant he wasn't chasing happiness but purpose. And it motivated her to try to do the same.

After finishing their prayer, Jamal grabbed his phone to check the latest news updates as had become his habit, especially since the beginning of Ramadan.

Hannah pulled off her prayer clothes and threw them into their basket, then went to the window to look outside. The street was dark and quiet.

'Hannah,' Jamal said loudly – too loudly for so early in the morning – making her jump.

'Shoosh!' she hissed. 'You'll wake Aya.'

He closed the bedroom door as he read aloud from his phone: 'Israeli media are reporting "cabinet-approved ceasefire brokered by Egypt". It goes into effect 2 am Friday.'

Hannah gasped.

'We have to be prepared. Remember 2014? They ended by destroying the high-rises. This round *began* with the high-rises.'

Jamal called his mother on WhatsApp. He couldn't connect. He sent her a message. He tried his sister. He couldn't connect. He sent her a message.

Hannah sat on the edge of the bed refreshing Twitter for updates. 'Ceasefire's just over three hours away,' she said. 'Apparently the airstrikes are pummelling Gaza now.'

'They'll want to take out as many as they can in the last hours.'

Jamal bashed out a tweet, reading aloud as he typed: 'Ceasefire but no end to the siege, no end to ethnic cleansing in Sheikh Jarrah, no end to occupation and apartheid. Just stop dropping bombs *for now* but carry on with the slow genocide. We need a ceasefire and an end to the colonial, apartheid stain on humanity that is the Zionist squatter state.'

'I am neutrally and objectively retweeting you in my mind,' Hannah said with an eyeroll.

Jamal's phone rang. It was his mother. They managed to speak for a few seconds before they lost connection. He had, at least, heard her voice.

31

Ashraf couldn't believe the trajectory he was on. A producer at the ABC's *Big Brief* radio program had reached out to him on his way to work (on a recommendation from Simon), inviting him to be interviewed on the program. They were interested in his Youth Power project and wanted to know, given student climate protests and recent tensions on the streets, his thoughts on engaging youth in political expression in a time of crisis and unrest.

So here he was doing the interview at his desk in his office during lunch.

The interviewer, Mark Adams, had a grammar-school accent (it was distinctive, you couldn't convince Ashraf otherwise) and spoke at a fast pace, like somebody being chased by a timer (which he guessed they were, given they had five minutes from the introduction to the end).

'So, Ash,' Mark started in a buoyant tone, after delivering an intro covering Black deaths in custody protests last month, student climate activists and young anti-Israel protesters. (*That was not in the brief,* Ashraf noted with alarm.)

'You've just been appointed to lead a new deradicalisation project with the Department of Home Affairs. Tell us about it.'

Ashraf quickly clarified that it was not a deradicalisation but an *empowerment* project. 'The project is about offering young people creative, resourceful and constructive ways to channel their feelings and grievances about overseas events and also find a way to' – and here he paused for greater effect – 'enact a politics of safe dissent and expression.'

Ashraf smiled to himself. He'd memorised that last bit from an article he'd read in *Journal for Deradicalization* and was impressed with how smoothly he was able to recall it without even referring to his detailed, highlighted notes.

'That's really important,' Mark said, 'because yesterday we saw students take the day off school to strike in cities across Australia and, in the past weeks, with the whole Israel–Hamas conflict we've seen huge protests on the streets – not just in Australia but all around the world. We've seen a teenager openly supporting Hamas in a university occupation. We've seen people burn the Israeli flag on the streets of Sydney, using problematic language such as calling Israel an apartheid state and shouting antisemitic chants. What do you think about that?'

'Well, of course, I condemn any expressions of antisemitism, Mark—'

'And we've seen debates about how democratic governments have to balance the right to protest with cracking down on hate speech.'

‘Yes, absolutely,’ Ashraf said, slightly flustered, unsure where Mark was going with his statements.

‘Turning to the Middle East,’ Mark continued, ‘which poses a different set of challenges to the climate strikes, governments also have to deal with the problem that vulnerable young people, who wouldn’t know much about the *huge* complexities of the decades-long Israel–Palestine conflict, beyond TikTok videos and, you know, social media, are potentially – I wouldn’t want to generalise – getting sucked into activist groups with their own agendas.’

Ashraf wasn’t sure when he was supposed to respond and simply hmmed, which he supposed conveyed agreement, and waited to be asked a question.

‘That Nabil student, for example,’ Mark said, ‘who was part of the occupation at your university.’

Ashraf felt his pulse quicken. But he had prepared some talking points under the heading *Nabil, University Protests.* He could manage this.

‘He was there with a group known for their anarchist activism,’ Mark said with unconcealed disdain. ‘I mean, he’s eighteen and legally an adult, but he’s just a high school student really and yet waving the Hamas flag and calling for attacks on Israel. It seems like a gross exploitation of a young person by a group that probably couldn’t have told you where Gaza is on the map a month ago. What are your thoughts?’

Ashraf cleared his throat and, grateful that this was not a video call, referred to his notes.

‘Well, Mark, you’ve raised some really important issues there. The right to protest is fundamental to our democratic values. But, of course, the discourse on rights is always complicated by competing rights.’

‘And the calls for boycotts? A PhD student and tutor at your university openly supported Nabil and called for a boycott of Israel. That singling out of Israel is pure antisemitism.’

‘Um, well, that’s a complicated issue, Mark. But let me circle back to your point on young people and activism. It’s reasonable to ask whether they have access to information to make informed choices, access to legal information and to understand the consequences of their actions. I can’t comment on Nabil’s case as I know only as much as you do. But as a member of JBU’s academic staff community, I’m concerned about the right of young people to be protected from activists who prey on their idealism and passion and don’t equip them with the knowledge to make informed decisions that will have lasting impacts on their futures.’

‘Yes, yes, exactly. To occupy a university building, to hold protests with antisemitic chants, to call for boycotts, divestment and sanctions from a university, a place that stands for intellectual enquiry and freedom of speech and the open exchange of ideas, is just mind-boggling. It seems a sure way to damage one’s cause rather than advance it. Thank you for your time today, Ash. Hope to have you on again in future – an update on your project, perhaps.’

32

Writing the feature together with Peter was, to Hannah's astonishment, a cooperative and smooth process. After visiting Al-Bayinnah, they'd spent a few hours in a spare office mapping out the shape of the piece, agreeing on the angle and overall structure, and then co-writing it.

The final article addressed the backlash on the school community, the impact on students and staff, the challenges faced by the principal to reassure her racialised students of their place in this country, and offered an insight, from Fayza's perspective as a principal, of the Islamic schooling system.

Intending to grab a coffee and clear her head, Hannah picked up her phone and took the lift down to the ground floor. Somewhere between the lift and the main doors, she realised her phone had been on silent and that she'd missed five calls and a text message from Jamal: *Call me ASAP.*

Aya.

She called Jamal in a sick panic.

'Is she okay?'

'What?' he asked, confused.

'Aya! Is she okay?'

'Yes, she's with your mum, remember?'

Hannah felt the nausea that had started rising slowly descend. She sat down on a retaining wall near the café. 'Are *you* okay?'

'Barnaby emailed me.'

'And?'

'He wants a meeting to discuss my social media posts. He mentioned a possible breach of university policies.'

Hannah closed her eyes and quietly exhaled. 'It's okay, habibi. We've got this,' Hannah reassured him, trying her best to control the tremor in her voice. 'They've got nothing. They're just trying to scare you. Probably a good idea to ask Ashraf to be your support person at the meeting.'

33

Ashraf was at his desk, caught up in a heated text exchange with Mya as he was listening to the playback of Mark Adams's program on his laptop, waiting for his segment to start. He hadn't realised that Mark had interviewed someone from the Zionist Executive Association of Australia right before him.

What's wrong with you? Mya texted. *How could you stoop so low? Fayza is so disappointed.*

It was astonishing that she would think that mattered to him.

Doesn't your neck hurt looking down at us all from your moral high ground? he bashed out in reply.

'What we saw at JBU was abhorrent,' the ZEAA spokesperson, whose name Ashraf hadn't caught, was telling Mark. 'We continue to call on the Australian Government to proscribe all of Hamas, an evil terrorist organisation whose tentacles reach so far that we have a high school student here at an Islamic school in Australia openly supporting them.'

Ashraf hit the mute button on his laptop because his office door was open but then, worried he'd miss his entry, turned the sound back on, opted instead to put the volume on minimum.

'Say what you want about me, but at least I'm not a sellout,' Mya wrote.

He could feel his anger rising.

'You're the one who sold everything we had to cosplay as a fanatic,' he sent back, then he slammed the phone on his desk.

There was an urgent knock on his door and he spotted Jamal. 'Come in,' Ashraf said and motioned for him to enter.

'Sorry to interrupt, Ashraf, but Barnaby's emailed me.'

He handed Ashraf his phone, which was open on the email.

'I have no idea how serious this is – if it'll impact my scholarship, my teaching position. Do you know what this could possibly mean?'

Ashraf finished reading and handed back the phone.

'I can't lose my scholarship, Ashraf,' Jamal said. 'The casual tutoring work. It's my livelihood.'

Ashraf was overcome by a sudden, powerful urge to scream. Hadn't he advised caution? Hadn't he told Jamal he couldn't take on the system? And now, look. Had Jamal's cleverly worded, intellectually superior grandstanding LinkedIn posts freed Gaza? Were his mother and sister safer now that he was facing a possible misconduct case?

Always acting with emotion, never intellect, never diplomacy or reason. It was the miserable fate of Arabs, indeed the Arab and Muslim world.

Ashraf forced himself to remain calm. First Mya (*Sellout*? Easy for her to virtue signal from her escape room of a village), and now Jamal. He just wanted to be left alone.

He cleared books and papers off a chair so that Jamal could sit down. Hearing his name, he hit pause on his laptop and Jamal apologised again for interrupting.

Ashraf waved his apology away. 'It's just my radio interview from this morning.'

'Oh, that's great. Where can I listen?'

'The playback's on the ABC website – it's today's *Big Brief*.' Ashraf pinched the bridge of his nose and closed his eyes. 'When is the meeting?'

'Tomorrow morning. Can you please … I'm sorry to ask, but I have no-one else. Can you please attend as my support person?'

'Maybe Leigh is better placed—'

'Please?' Jamal pressed. 'I'd prefer you.'

Ashraf nodded his agreement, not trusting himself to keep the reproach out of his voice. *I don't have much choice, do I?*

34

Hannah spent most of her bus trip to the office catching up on her multiple group chats, scrolling through Twitter and ordering groceries. When she'd finished, she leant her head against the window, remembering the calmness of her morning with Jamal. They'd woken early, prayed fajr and made dua together. They'd remained kneeled on the prayer mat as Jamal called his mother and sister and Hannah read the Quran.

She treasured that pre-dawn ritual, when her world was quiet and still, and she could recite حَسْبُنَا ٱللَّهُ وَنِعْمَ ٱلْوَكِيلُ, *Allah is sufficient for us, and the best disposer of affairs.* It fortified her for the day ahead. And as many times a day as she failed to remember those words and succumbed to despair or anger, she always had her prayer mat to return to the next morning with Jamal by her side.

Her moment of calm was interrupted by a message from Jeanette. It was a link to an article in *The Chronicle* accompanied by an angry emoji.

Hannah felt her breath catch in her throat. She opened the link.

Peter had, under a solo byline this time, written a second article about Al-Bayinnah. Actually, not an article – an 'exclusive feature'.

The Israel–Hamas War: A tale of two schools

Hannah steeled herself and read the opening paragraphs.

> Since the arrest of Nabil Mostafa, a student at Al-Bayinnah, an Islamic school in Western Sydney, there has been a wave of negative attention on faith-based schools.
>
> What is their role in a secular multicultural society? How do global conflicts infiltrate local contexts? But perhaps these debates miss the point.
>
> Against the backdrop of the Israel–Palestine conflict, and the loss of Jewish and Palestinian lives, there has been a rise in antisemitism and Islamophobia in Australia. And it is faith-based schools that have stepped in to offer Jewish and Muslim students a safe space.

'What the fuck,' she said aloud.

It was the strangest sensation, to be sitting in a bus, travelling across the Anzac Bridge, sliding slightly across the seat, completely numb. As Hannah focused on breathing in and out, that numbness was replaced by a building rage.

She read on. Al-Bayinnah was not, it was now clear, the only school Peter had visited. He'd also visited Zion Academic College, and the feature was a profile of both schools, focusing on how *distressed and traumatised Jewish and Muslim students find healing and solidarity in their school communities.*

He'd quoted staff at Zion Academic College and repurposed quotes from Fayza, obtained during their visit, about how hard they were all working to *support students watching the conflict overseas.*

Peter wrote:

> At Al-Bayinnah, students are engaged in bake sales and communal prayers, and speakers are invited to counsel students about the impact of the war.

Meanwhile, at Zion Academic College:

> Students in primary school make greeting cards with messages to IDF soldiers, some of whom are related to students and staff at the school. They're treated to guest talks by alumni who have served in the IDF.

The article continued:

> Motifs and symbols are core elements in helping students find a strong sense of identity and belonging.

At Al-Bayinnah, the Palestinian flag features in many artworks around the school and is even held by a mannequin child (covered up conservatively in a hijab).

At Zion Academic College, the Australian flag flies high, but the Israeli flag can be found all around the school, including in posters for youth exchange programs to Israel and parent information sessions on opportunities for aliya (immigration to Israel).

Both schools are a testament to the endurance of faith communities and the way they rally together to offer marginalised students a safe space to connect to their faith, as Muslims, and their homeland, as Jews.

Hannah would lose her job over this because there was just no way she could remain quiet.

How dare they? she screamed internally as she disembarked at her stop and crossed the road to her building. *How fucking dare he write this? How fucking dare John publish it?*

She wanted to set a match to a printed copy in front of them.

When Hannah arrived at work, she stormed into the lift. As soon as the doors opened, she charged down the corridor to find Peter in the kitchen, alone, spreading butter on raisin toast.

'A tale of two schools?' she asked, her voice quivering with anger.

He smiled – just for a microsecond, like a child expecting praise – but then he registered the anger that seemed to have drained all colour from her face and adjusted his own expression, settling on a confused frown.

Dear, merciful God, she thought. *He's proud.*

'Hi, Hannah,' Peter said, with a tone of curiosity and concern.

Her hands were shaking, so she planted them straight down by her sides to steady herself. 'I don't understand how you could write this,' she said, trying so hard to be careful with her words.

'I thought you'd be happy with it,' he explained, eyebrows raised in genuine surprise. 'It adds even more nuance and perspective to Al-Bayinnah. It *honours* the amazing work they're doing for students.'

'Are you serious?'

Hannah threw her hands in the air in exasperation.

'Cupcake fundraisers are *not* the same as cards to the Israeli *Occupation* Forces! This is not a Jewish–Muslim issue! Palestinians haven't *lost* their lives! Over two hundred people – sixty-six *children*, Peter – have been killed by Israeli bombs! You do *not* get to describe that as the loss of Palestinian and Jewish lives. You do *not* get to two-sides a nuclear, US-armed occupier and an occupied refugee population! You do *not* get to equate the coloniser with the colonised!'

'I don't appreciate your aggressive tone,' Peter said, now indignant. He spoke to her as though to a hysterical child. 'Let's talk when you've calmed down.'

He picked up his toast and walked out.

Hannah burst into tears. She'd crossed the line. She was his institutional subordinate. Hierarchically, she had the right to perhaps one passive-aggressive mutter a week – certainly not an angry outburst. How could she be so reckless?

This was no place to cry, not in a kitchen exposed by glass walls and doors. She dashed to the bathroom, keeping her head down, and stood in front of the sink, washing off her smudged mascara. She patted her face dry and, hearing steps approaching the door, locked herself in a cubicle.

She shot off an email to Fayza, explaining that she had nothing to do with Peter's article and that she found the framing appalling. She took deep breaths, emerging only when she was sure she had control over her voice and tears.

She passed John's office and noticed that Peter was in there too.

As she sat down in her cubicle, her email pinged with a reply from Fayza:

> There wasn't a single line in that article that would lead me to think it was attributable to you. Thank you again for your article yesterday and for all your efforts. I can see what you're up against. You're doing an incredible job.

No, no, no! Hannah didn't want to cry *again*. Her nose prickled. Her head pounded. She grabbed two tablets of Panadol from her drawer and washed them down with a swig from an old bottle of water.

Her inbox pinged with an email from John.

Dear Hannah,

I want to reassure you that we are here to support you through these difficult times and that we all care about your wellbeing.

Please remember that you have 24/7 access to our confidential Employee Assistance Program.

Kind regards,
John

Hannah would have preferred to have been disciplined.

She slammed her laptop shut and walked to the lifts. She needed to get out of the office.

As she emerged onto the street, it hit her: she couldn't do this anymore. She wanted to resign. She let out a bitter laugh – that's if she wasn't sacked first. But, no, they were clever enough to know that would be messy. The optics would be bad. Too much reputational risk for the paper.

But how could she resign? How could she throw away this opportunity? She was the only Arab and Muslim journalist at *The Chronicle*. Hannah felt not only the burden of representation but also the burden of mere existence. And yet, for every shitty moment, every indignity and racist encounter, she felt a responsibility to persevere. This was an opportunity any other journalist of colour would crave.

And where would she go? What independent media in this white colony would offer her work that could pay her bills and let her inform beyond the already informed?

She was tired. So, so tired.

She found a bench at Hyde Park and sat down.

Allah is sufficient for us, and the best disposer of affairs, she recited, over and over again.

35

Barnaby sat at the head of an oval table with Astrid, the HR manager, beside him, her fingers poised over a MacBook ready to take notes. Astrid, who'd always struck Ashraf as too placid and conflict-averse for an HR role, was smiling widely, as if trying to inject some zen into what everyone knew were unpleasant circumstances.

Barnaby and Ashraf engaged in some small talk: Ashraf's media interview ('Excellent outreach, Ash'), the student rallies on climate change ('This generation is just so impressive,' said Barnaby, to which Ashraf replied, 'Oh, yes! The world is in good hands!') and how busy they were ('Is it just me or does the admin load increase every year?' Barnaby joked).

There was a short pause, punctuated by some nervous shuffling from Astrid. Jamal still hadn't said a word.

Ashraf politely suggested they start the meeting. Barnaby seemed relaxed, which was surely a good sign that there might be a way to de-escalate whatever trouble Jamal was in.

Barnaby opened by informing Jamal that the university had received formal complaints in relation to two of Jamal's social media posts.

Jamal, arms folded across his chest and one leg jiggling up and down. 'Which posts exactly?' he asked.

Barnaby gestured to Astrid and she tilted the MacBook to face him. Barnaby put his glasses on and squinted at the screen. 'The first offending post was made on 10 March, I beg your pardon, 10 May on LinkedIn. You stated: "There can be no co-existence with Zionism. Zionism is racism. Nothing less than dismantling the Zionist state. It has and never had a right to exist."'

Barnaby paused, looked at Jamal, whose face remained expressionless, and continued.

'The second post was a video you posted. Astrid, can you please bring that up on the screen?'

'Yes, sure. Oops, I accidentally closed the tab – one second, please.'

Astrid fumbled with the laptop and once again turned the screen to face Barnaby.

'So, this post was made on 15 May, also on your LinkedIn,' Barnaby said, his tone polite, almost convivial. 'It's a clip from a speech you appear to be giving at a protest. The complaints are in relation to the t-shirt you're wearing, the content of the speech and your caption. I believe the caption is in fact a transcription of the video clip?'

He looked to Jamal for clarification.

‘I post quite frequently,’ Jamal said drily. ‘You’ll have to show me the post for me to be able to answer you.’

‘Yes, of course,’ Barnaby said, turning the MacBook to face Jamal and Ashraf.

Jamal leant forward, scanned the screen and leant back again. ‘Yes, the caption transcribes what I said, which is: “Nothing less than the end to the Zionist state and a free Palestine of equals from the river to the sea.”’

Ashraf felt himself wince.

Barnaby removed his glasses, placed them on the table in front of him and looked up. ‘The complainants characterise your posts as antisemitic, threatening and racially vilifying, which exposes you to a potential breach of both the student and staff codes of conduct.’

Ashraf glanced at Jamal who sat, unperturbed, arms still folded across his chest. *Like somebody*, he thought angrily, *who doesn’t want a problem to go away.*

Jamal flashed a wry smile. ‘I’m not sure I understand what’s going on here,’ he said. ‘My posts are directed at a political ideology and a state. Can you racially vilify a state? An ideology?’

‘The complainants felt victimised and threatened,’ Barnaby replied.

‘Who are the complainants?’

‘That’s confidential.’

‘Well, are they JBU students? Staff? Random people who follow my LinkedIn?’

'As I said, that's confidential.'

'If I'm being accused of antisemitism and racial vilification, then surely I'm entitled to know the racial identity of my accuser?'

Barnaby spoke carefully. 'These complaints have been made … and we are giving you the opportunity to respond … and to clarify how your posts are not in breach of JBU's policies.'

'But how do I answer the allegations if I don't know who is making them?'

'We respect the confidentiality of the complainants.'

'But their racial identity is key to the allegations.'

Barnaby didn't respond.

Ashraf realised, though he would never admit it aloud, that the meeting belonged in a Kafka novel.

'Okay, so I'm being accused of antisemitism.' Jamal sat up straighter and continued, 'Are the complainants Jewish?'

'As I said, they have specifically asked to remain anonymous.'

'Assuming they're Jewish, which you won't confirm, there's nothing I posted or said at the rally that attacks Jewish people or the Jewish faith. My oppressor, as a Palestinian, is my occupier and coloniser, Israel, and its political ideology of Zionism.'

'We're going round in circles,' Barnaby said.

Ashraf detected a hint of weariness in Barnaby's tone. He didn't seem particularly invested in the complaint.

His speech now was clinical, void of any emotion. In Ashraf's assessment, Barnaby seemed to view the whole matter as one of great inconvenience. And Jamal was too bloody obstinate to realise that was a blessing.

Barnaby was looking for a way out, Ashraf was sure of it. Some contrition, something that would let him tick a box and confirm the situation had been dealt with. What degree of naivety did it require for Jamal to actually think that *oppressor*, *occupier*, *coloniser* were words that meant anything to Barnaby.

My God, Ashraf thought. *Isn't it the left that bleats on about not appealing to power on moral terms?*

'You've made these posts,' Barnaby tried again. 'You don't deny you did, and I'm telling you there are people who were threatened and felt vilified and unsafe.'

'My posts were directed at Zionism, a political ideology, and Israel, a settler-colonial state,' Jamal said clearly. 'A racial vilification claim only makes sense if Zionism is being treated as a religious or ethnic identity. That's like saying Marxism or socialism or communism are identity categories. By that logic, communists can claim the status of a protected category of identity on the basis that there are Chinese communists who feel threatened by critiques of communism.'

Ashraf, sensing Jamal was not going to back down, knew he had to interrupt. Maybe the way out was to zoom in on technicalities.

'Barnaby, can you just clarify, please, why Jamal's social media posts, which were made in his personal capacity, breach the codes of conduct?'

'They were not made in his personal capacity,' Barnaby said. 'Jamal's LinkedIn profile explicitly associates him with JBU.' He turned to Jamal. 'You specifically mention you study and work at JBU. Your posts also, arguably, bring the university into disrepute. Hence your posts fall under the student and staff codes of conduct.'

'So, when I advocate for Palestine, I should do so in a personal capacity and not mention JBU or exercise my right to academic freedom?'

Ashraf noticed that Astrid was furiously typing notes.

Barnaby took a moment to respond, settling on: 'You should be careful and comment in, er, a personal capacity.'

Ashraf saw an opportunity and jumped in again. 'I think we can nip this in the bud, then' he said. 'Jamal can remove the references to JBU on all his social media accounts and ensure that, in any public advocacy or social media engagement involving Palestine, he doesn't associate himself with JBU.'

Barnaby's expression shifted. Was that relief in his eyes?

Ashraf felt emboldened in his assessment that this was a situation in which management was seeking a way to flex its authority and save face.

He looked hopefully at Jamal. 'Would you agree to that?' he asked.

'And to delete the posts?' Barnaby added. 'I think that would draw a line under the matter.'

'And if a line isn't drawn?' Jamal asked.

'We will have to, um, consider your position, and ... next steps.'

Jamal sat in sullen silence for longer than was comfortable. Then, quite unexpectedly, he laughed. 'Like a conversation between the sword and the neck,' he said.

Of course, Ashraf understood the reference, but Barnaby stared back at Jamal blankly, not a hint of curiosity on his sallow face. Astrid smiled again.

Jamal took a few more moments before speaking again. Looking directly at Barnaby, he asked: 'If I delete the posts and remove JBU from my profile, will there be a record on my file that this matter was finalised in my favour?'

Barnaby addressed Astrid. 'Well, um, we will record that it was not taken further.'

Jamal took out his phone, opened LinkedIn, scrolled down to the posts and deleted them, deleted JBU from his profile, then flipped the phone around to show them all.

Jamal stood up and left the room. Ashraf followed close behind. They took the lift in silence down to the main foyer and walked out of the building.

'That was a wise decision,' Ashraf said, trying to mask his relief and appear sympathetic to Jamal's predicament. 'It went well, all things considered. The university could have doubled down.'

'I listened to your interview.'

Ashraf beamed, but his face dropped when he saw Jamal wasn't smiling.

'We don't have the right to international law, boycotts, sanctions, divestment, protests, chants, marches, social media posts. So, tell me, will our liberation happen through Change.org or a bake-for-Palestine fundraiser?'

'Look, I know you're upset, but your PhD and teaching are safe, Jamal. You won.'

Jamal's eyes flashed. 'Yes, I won. They aren't getting rid of me that easily. That's not the point though. If everything about our resistance is taboo now, nothing from our oppressors will be taboo later.'

He turned and walked away, leaving Ashraf standing alone.

36

Hannah was still in Hyde Park. She'd tried to call Jamal, but his phone kept going straight to voicemail, suggesting he was still in the meeting with Barnaby and Ashraf. She messaged him to call her as soon as he was free.

She'd finally managed to steady her breathing and was now taking in the scene around her, the long avenue of weeping figs, the sound of birds above.

A group of teenage boys in school uniform passed her. They were falling over each other in laughter, oblivious to the people around them, wrapped up in their own exuberance.

She held back a laugh as one of them suddenly climbed onto another's back, yelping, before they both collapsed onto the ground in a fit of giggles.

Hannah's mind wandered to Nabil. All the words written about him, around him, because of him and not a single word *from* him. He'd become a piece of velcro, stuck with other people's assumptions, labels, narratives and accusations.

She remembered a Mahmoud Darwish quote her father would often shout at the screen whenever some traitor leader was on *Al Jazeera*: *I don't know who sold the homeland, but I know who paid the price.*

How many sales were each of them making every damn day in exchange for working inside the system? How many of their transactions were being paid for by those who had the least? When would they have to face the cost of their self-censorship and compromise?

Khalas. Enough.

Her phone started ringing. She answered to hear Jamal, to her surprise, laughing.

'Are you okay?' she asked.

'Yeah, habibti.'

'What happened?'

Instead of telling her about the meeting, Jamal began talking about Bassel al-Araj, a revolutionary activist who was assassinated by Israel in 2017.

'He was obsessed with books, knowledge, disobedience,' he told Hannah. 'He developed a theory called *ishtibak*, entanglement and creative disruption. Instead of confronting your enemy on their terms, meeting them where they want, you create sites of tension and disruption.'

'Okay,' Hannah said.

'I deleted the posts. But I'll post them again, across different platforms, in creative ways. I'll keep writing, teaching and disrupting. I'm a child of Gaza. Do they think a white mediocre manager named *Barnaby* is going to get the better of me?'

Hannah knew then that she wouldn't resign. She would return to work and face them. Isn't that what the 'Manifesto of Dignity and Hope' that youth activists released a few days ago in Palestine was all about? She would have her meltdown and return, and she would make trouble, cause insurrections, tell the truth.

Hannah jumped up. She had to get back to the office. She would ignore Peter and throw herself into her work.

'I can meet you at your office tonight,' said Jamal. 'There's a candlelight vigil on the Opera House steps. Do you want to head over together?'

Jamal messaged her around five o'clock: *I'm downstairs with Aya. Still up for the vigil? Tianna says there are cops there already, but our crowd is growing. Mostly families.*

Hannah sent a thumbs up in reply. She grabbed her bag, jacket and phone, and squeezed into a packed lift that took her down to the ground floor.

Jamal was waiting near the cab rank with Aya who was sleeping in her pram. He was wearing his *Zionism is Fascism* t-shirt, a keffiyeh wrapped around his neck. His face lit up when he saw her.

She rushed to him, and they embraced each other tightly. She planted a soft kiss on Aya's cheek and then stepped back suddenly and grabbed his keffiyeh.

'Can I borrow this, please?' Hannah asked.

'Yeah, sure. I've got another one in my bag.'

She threw her handbag into the bottom of the pram, ran back into the building and caught the lift, empty this time, up to her floor.

When the lift dinged open, Peter looked up from his cubicle, puzzled, having seen her leave only moments before. Defiant, Hannah stared back and strode to her desk.

When she reached her cubicle, she shook open the keffiyeh and draped it over her chair. She could feel Peter's eyes on her still, but she walked back to the lifts, head held high.

When the doors opened again on the ground floor, Hannah rushed to Jamal and Aya. Without a word, they started walking in the direction of Circular Quay, Hannah pushing the pram, each lost in their own thoughts.

On the way, Aya woke up and started calling, 'Mama.'

Hannah stopped the pram, unbuckled Aya and took her into her arms, smothering her with kisses. She balanced Aya on her hip and motioned for Jamal to push the pram.

They walked on and Hannah's mind wandered to a recent image out of Gaza that had transfixed her. That of a little Palestinian boy and girl – cousins, it was reported – grinning widely as they stood in rubble and debris, holding the pet fish they saved in a jar after their home was destroyed by an Israeli airstrike.

She'd seen comments online celebrating the 'resilience' of Palestinian children. It infuriated her, this fetishisation of resilience. Be resilient over a paper cut or losing your Barbie, not over dismembered classmates or shredded parents. She couldn't bear the pontificating of those who expected superhuman resilience from occupied, bombed and traumatised children.

No, it wasn't resilience that she was thinking about as they walked past the magisterial St Mary's Cathedral and Aya squeezed Hannah's cheek with her chubby hands. The image of the children with their pet fish had affected her for other reasons.

Hannah was ashamed to admit, even to herself, that she had grown accustomed to encountering Palestinian children, not as children, but as targets – either killed or waiting to be killed. But that photo revealed something more. It showed two children momentarily claiming a space of childlike normality. She felt humbled. How happy they looked, standing on their demolished home, proudly holding their goldfish in a jar of dirty water.

She would never stop fighting for them.

Not for the sake of their humanity but for the sake of her own.

Acknowledgements

I acknowledge [redacted] and [redacted], working in the universities of [redacted] and [redacted] and the media establishments of [redacted] and [redacted], who exchanged texts, phone calls, emails with me as I did my research for this book. I acknowledge the insights, experiences, anecdotes and incidents you generously shared with me.

You know who you are.

I acknowledge that, due to a feckless academic and journalist class, revealing your names or the identity of your workplaces would invite your own discipline and punishment. I acknowledge your fortitude, integrity and commitment to working within establishments that dehumanise you every single day. I acknowledge you for speaking and acting despite the personal costs, and I acknowledge your courage for taking the moral path, not the safe one.

There were people who tried to stop this book from being published. They failed. This was possible because of the staunch, utterly unshakeable solidarity and sacrifices that Blak, brown, and anti-Zionist Jewish peers, friends and allies were prepared to make without hesitation. Over fifty UQP authors wrote to UQP to express their solidarity with me. You know who you are, thank you. Thank you in particular to Sara Saleh, Omar Sakr, Tony Birch, Melissa Lucashenko, Michael Mohammed Ahmed and Samah Sabawi. You know what you did. The universe also knows, and kindness, integrity and generosity always pay forward.

Would this book exist without Aviva Tuffield? I doubt it. Publishing in such a time takes talent, vision and courage, and Aviva you have it all. Thank you. Thank you to the UQP team for believing in this story, in artistic freedom, and for all your efforts to bring *Discipline* out to the world. Thank you to Amani Haydar for your dazzling artwork. Your talent never ceases to amaze me. And thank you to Amy Daoud for your gorgeous cover design. Thank you to Lauren Mitchell for your excellent copyediting. Your meticulous attention to detail and my lack of it made for a perfect team. Thank you to Bassam Abun-Nadi for your sharp and clever insights and feedback on the first draft, and to my sister, Nada, who always picks up my silly mistakes and relishes doing so as all younger sisters should.

They say that life imitates art. In my case, art couldn't catch up with my life. It's been a dystopian ride, but I've been on it with family and friends, and I am indebted to them all but especially to the love of my life, Ibrahim, and to my dear friends and colleagues, especially [redacted] and [redacted].

Thank you, above all, to my readers. May we remain undisciplined. It is the only hope for this broken world.

Randa Abdel-Fattah is an ARC Future Fellow at Macquarie University. Her research areas cover Islamophobia, race, Palestine, the war on terror, youth identities and social movement activism. Dr Abdel-Fattah is also a former lawyer and the award-winning author of twelve books for children and young adults, which have been translated into over thirteen languages.

She has won and been shortlisted and longlisted for awards including the Australian Book Industry Award, the Australian Book of the Year Award, the Stella Prize, and the Miles Franklin Literary Award. *Discipline* is Abdel-Fattah's debut adult novel and was due to be featured at the 2026 Adelaide Festival's Writer's Week before her disinvitation sparked a mass author boycott that led to the festival's cancellation.